GW00686112

Shell
Beach

Books by Davis Bunn

Miramar Bay
Firefly Cove
Moondust Lake
Tranquility Falls
The Cottage on Lighthouse Lane
The Emerald Tide
Shell Beach

Novellas
The Christmas Hummingbird

DAVIS BUNN

Shell
Beach

KENSINGTON
PUBLISHING CORP.

www.kensingtonbooks.com

This book is a work of fiction. Names, characters, businesses, organizations, places, events, and incidents either are the product of the author's imagination or are used fictitiously. Any resemblance to actual persons, living or dead, events, or locales is entirely coincidental.

To the extent that the image or images on the cover of this book depict a person or persons, such person or persons are merely models, and are not intended to portray any character or characters featured in the book.

KENSINGTON BOOKS are published by

Kensington Publishing Corp.
119 West 40th Street
New York, NY 10018

Copyright © 2023 by Davis Bunn

All rights reserved. No part of this book may be reproduced in any form or by any means without the prior written consent of the Publisher, excepting brief quotes used in reviews.

All Kensington titles, imprints, and distributed lines are available at special quantity discounts for bulk purchases for sales promotion, premiums, fund-raising, educational, or institutional use. Special book excerpts or customized printings can also be created to fit specific needs. For details, write or phone the office of the Kensington Special Sales Manager: Attn. Special Sales Department. Kensington Publishing Corp., 119 West 40th Street, New York, NY 10018. Phone: 1-800-221-2647.

Library of Congress Card Catalogue Number: 2022950818

The K with book logo Reg. U.S. Pat. & TM Off.

ISBN: 978-1-4967-3470-9
First Kensington Hardcover Edition: May 2023

ISBN: 978-1-4967-3471-6 (ebook)

10 9 8 7 6 5 4 3 2 1

Printed in the United States of America

This Book Is Dedicated To:

Nancy Smith
Bunny Matthews

Paulyn Agyemang
Joana Haizel
Kaditu Kargbo
Heather Sweet

Baxter Home Health
Hospice of the Chesapeake

Becky's friends to the end.

Shell
Beach

CHAPTER 1

Around four that morning, Noah Hearst decided he'd tossed and turned long enough. He ate a final breakfast at the rental apartment's kitchen sink, staring at his reflection in the darkened window. Took his last bag down to the Ford double cab. Stood there in the quiet and the dark for a long moment. Wondering if he would ever make it back to Los Angeles. And if so, why.

Then he headed north.

Clearing out his former office had gone more smoothly than he'd expected. Eight and a half years of sweat and tears and very hard days had been reduced to one truckload of boxes and records and plans and models. He should probably have thrown it all away, but just then found it hard enough to watch the movers shift his life into two self-storage units and then lock the metal doors.

Clearing out what was now his ex-wife's home had been far easier. Three and a half years of temporary separations and endless counseling sessions meant he had already shifted most things into a series of rentals. That final day, his wife safely removed from the scene, Noah had only half-a-pickup's worth of items still to pack. When he was done, Noah gave his former home the sort of look that could only come from an emotional distance. The pale marble floors, the carefully chosen furniture, the drapes over the rear windows that had cost him almost twenty thousand dollars. It had always been Elaine's place, somewhere Noah visited between gigs.

That previous afternoon, Noah had found himself taking a slow tour of the artwork, pausing long enough to recall the nasty arguments they'd had over some of the items. The prices, sure, they had been good for some yells. But really it had mostly come down to the art itself. Noah had thought them aimless and angry. Now, he suspected Elaine's intention was to cover their walls with colorful indictments that he would never give her what she needed from their relationship.

Nine years in Los Angeles and Noah had never been farther north than Santa Barbara. When he needed a break and had the time, he had done what Elaine wanted. The islands were top of her wish list, Kauai in particular. Noah had disliked feeling so cut off from his work and all the problems he worried over leaving behind. Elaine, in turn, had despised how he couldn't just release and let go. Such arguments always came down to him reminding his wife that these worries were how he paid for the five-star hotel, and her response had been to . . .

With a start, Noah realized he had driven all the way to Long Beach, accompanied by the circular tirade that had dominated his homelife for far too long. Which was good for a bitter smile. Driving north, the remnants of his previous existence packed in boxes that filled his pickup. Arguing with a woman who was doing her best to put him firmly in the past. Which was what he should be doing as well.

The sun rose as he passed Santa Barbara's northernmost exit and entered new terrain. Amos, his sort-of half brother, had been pressing him to make this trip for six years. Ever since they had finally broken the commands of two sets of parents and connected. But by the time they were communicating, Noah's world did not permit such excursions. Thankfully, Amos liked coming down to Los Angeles, despite the fact that he and Noah's ex were definitely oil and water. Amos was the sheriff whose territory contained the farmlands and small communities between Miramar and San Luis Obispo. He was tall, rangy, soft-spoken, and half Black.

When Noah was two, his mother had fallen in love with an African American dentist and left her former life behind. A fact Noah's father did not divulge until his only son was in his teens. And even then, his father failed to mention the reason for the swift departure was that she was already pregnant with Amos.

Noah had been raised in Phoenix by a good dad and a great mom. He never revealed to them that he and Amos had met and discovered that despite the fact they had virtually nothing in common, they had bonded. From that very first moment.

After the two failed attempts to make peace between Elaine and Amos, the brothers started meeting in Santa Barbara, where Amos had friends with a boat. A number of the boats moored in Santa Barbara's harbor were owned by collectives. One of these groups had members who owed Amos for situations he refused to divulge. Amos never discussed his work. He loved hearing Noah talk about Hollywood and the stress of meeting one deadline after another. The stars who scarcely knew Noah existed. The tyrants called directors. Penny-pinching producers. Network chiefs. All the people Noah was now leaving behind. Amos relished the hours spent listening to Noah. He said it was like being introduced to a tribe of Martians. But in their six years of meeting up, Amos had never once spoken about his own work.

The boat was no great shakes, a thirty-six-foot Hatteras that had seen better days. It was poorly maintained by owners who preferred to leave a good cleaning to the next person. Amos had found it mildly hilarious how Noah had to be ordered not to clean up after men he had never met.

What neither man had expected, certainly not Noah, was how much he loved being on the sea.

He had never owned a boat. Never been on a cruise. The brothers went out only when the sea was utterly flat. The roll of even medium-size swells had Amos leaning over the side. Noah was bitterly disappointed when weather or waves kept them in port. He loved the open vista. For weeks after each outing, he dreamed of sparkling waters, of dolphins who accompanied them out into the endless blue.

On the nearly perfect days, they cruised the Channel Islands, choosing a lonely cove, anchoring for a meal, swimming in the frigid waters, motoring home sunburnt and salty.

Just loving it.

In the hard, lonely months, Noah found great solace in recalling those moments. Sitting in court, dealing with lawyers, watching his corporate dreams turn to dust as well, his only real comfort came from knowing another boat ride was beckoning.

The dream of having his own boat, going wherever he wished, often seemed more real than the disaster his life had become. Such yearnings became a healing balm, a silent plea for better days once the nightmares were over and done.

As he passed the Santa Barbara exits, Noah resisted the urge to drive down to the harbor and have a second breakfast at his favorite diner, watching the boats sparkle and beckon in the sunrise. But Amos was waiting for him, so he followed his almost-brother's directions north, past Lompoc and San Luis Obispo, taking the smaller state road through the farmlands and the valleys, into the gathering light of a brand-new day.

Amos and his wife lived in a country-style collective of homes eleven miles south of the Miramar town limits. The development had been started by the children of a rancher. Together with a local contractor, they built homes for people like themselves. Families who loved the country but had no interest in working the land. The lots were generous, the homes low-slung, the owners mostly blue collar and quietly proud of their way of life.

Amos greeted Noah as he always did, solemnly shaking hands, asking about his trip. The house was empty, his two daughters in school, his wife at work. Amos wore his sheriff's uniform, minus the hat and heavy belt and gear. On his feet were scruffy house slippers. "Frittatas and biscuits work for you?"

"Sounds great." Two places were set at the battered kitchen table. "Sorry I haven't made it up here until now."

"You've been busy."

Those were the last words spoken until both finished eating. That was another thing Noah shared with the man. How Amos clearly disliked casual chatter. If they had something important to say, well, out with it. Otherwise the quiet worked just fine.

Amos set their empty plates in the sink, recharged their mugs, and led Noah to the backyard. When they had settled into a pair of rickety lawn chairs, and Noah had given a few grateful moments to the rising wind off the unseen Pacific and the birdsong, Noah said, "You saw this coming."

"I was afraid it might, sure enough."

"You never cared for Elaine."

"I didn't need to. She wasn't my wife." Amos sipped from

his mug, set it on the grass. "In my job, you see a few people at their best, and a lot more at their very worst. You learn to read a situation fast, especially if there's danger involved. Watching for the unseen blade, the gun hiding behind the smile."

Noah stared at the angular gentleman seated next to him. All the time they had spent together, these were the first words Amos had ever spoken about his life on the road.

Amos went on. "You're wrong, what I thought of Elaine. I knew she didn't approve of me. So I took a giant step back. All the same, I saw how things weren't getting better between you two, the emotional bruises you carried most times we met. I've been concerned she was going to break your heart. That she'd feel like it was her right to hit you at your lowest point. Like you deserved to be crushed. So no, I didn't dislike her then. But I sure do now."

"Maybe I did deserve it."

"And maybe your job in life isn't to be perfect, but to do your best. Did you?"

"I tried. Given the circumstances. Hard as I could. I tried."

"Elaine is a lady who wants her man to treat her like she's the center of her universe. That's what would keep her happy."

Noah thought of Elaine's parents, the way her father had doted on both his girls. Right to his last breath. "I guess I knew that all along."

"That's not your nature. It never has been. You've got dreams of your own. Goals that had nothing to do with what Elaine wanted. She was jealous of your dreams. She saw them as competition."

Noah rubbed the spot over his aching heart and watched the cottonwood trees weave scripts in the rising wind. "I loved her. So much."

"I know you did."

"Truth be told, I still do."

Amos waved a hand, like he was swatting at passing shadows. "You want my opinion, it's time to move on."

"Elaine would probably agree with you."

"See, it's not about her anymore. Which is what I want to talk with you about. When you're ready to listen."

Noah heard the sharp tone. The sort of edge a father might use on a son who was leaning toward that wrong and fateful step. He wanted to shout at the man, challenge Amos's right to talk down like that. Treat his hurt as trivial. Or whatever.

Noah rose from his chair and took a slow circuit around the yard. The family's massive mixed-breed came over and gave him a careful sniff, then drifted away. He knew his rage had little to do with Amos and his words. It was all about someone finally telling him what he needed to hear. Noah could almost hear the links to his past being broken. The life he wanted to claim. The worlds he wanted to conquer. Gone. Whether he liked it or not.

When he was ready, Noah returned to his chair. Not liking what the man had said, nor his manner. Barking like a cop. Not liking it one bit.

But that didn't mean Noah wasn't in need of just that sort of message.

Amos took Noah's return as his time to ask, "What are you planning on doing now?"

Noah replied, "You know what I've been hoping."

"A boat. A trip. Come back when you're good and ready. I know."

"Between giving Elaine half of everything, and not getting nearly what I deserve for the company, that dream is just another thing I've left in my rearview mirror."

"You sure about that, are you?"

"Pretty certain, yeah." He leaned over and retrieved his mug. "Buying a boat is only the start of what it costs. And the kind of seagoing vessel I was after . . ."

"Expensive."

"Out of reach."

"Not to mention how you'll need a place to live. When you decide to spend a night on steady ground. Where folks are meant to be."

Noah had the distinct impression Amos had tucked a smile firmly out of sight. "Where are you going with this?"

He rose to his feet. "What say you and I take a ride."

CHAPTER 2

The San Luis Obispo police storage unit was located in arid scrubland south of the Morro Bay main highway. Buildings and warehouses and acres of equipment were rimmed by rusting metal fence and razor wire. Though why anyone would want to break into this place was beyond Noah. As they rose from Amos's Wagoneer, dry desert heat struck at him from all sides. "What are we doing here?"

"There's someone you need to meet." Amos leaned through his open door and beeped his horn. "Here he comes now."

A solid man with steel-gray hair and a gut that defied his jacket's buttons emerged from the nearest concrete structure. "*Cabrón!*"

"Zia Morales, meet my brother, Noah Hearst."

The man's stride revealed a gold detective badge attached to his gun belt. A matching gold tooth glinted when he smiled. "Amos, my man, I hate to be the one to tell you, but this guy, he's Anglo."

"Nobody's perfect."

The man's grip was iron hard. "Amos tells me I'm looking at another addict."

"He means you like boats."

"Like doesn't go far enough," Noah said.

"That's what I want to hear." To Amos, "You tell him what we've got?"

"I figured he'd probably run for the hills if I did."

"Yeah, there's definitely some crazy attached to this." The tooth caught the sunlight a second time. "But hey. Nobody sane owns a boat, am I right?"

"Crazy works for me," Noah replied.

"A man after my own heart." Zia stripped off his jacket and dropped it in Amos's car. "Right this way."

Their stroll across the cracked concrete was marked by the constant *pop-pop* of gunfire. "Gun range," Zia said. "Latest crop of recruits are busy missing targets."

Amos asked, "We safe here?"

"Hard to say," Zia replied. "They're supposed to be aiming in the other direction. But you know recruits."

Their destination was the compound's largest structure, a massive warehouse whose entrance was a full thirty feet high and twice as broad. The shadows offered a semblance of coolness. When Noah's eyes adjusted to the dark, he froze.

"Welcome to the police auction hall," Zia told him. "Like I said, crazy."

The building was littered with an odd array of equipment and vehicles, including two tractor-trailers, four Dodge Chargers, a pair of rusting Explorers, and a derelict mobile home.

And looming over everything was a boat.

The yacht was huge. It occupied the warehouse's central position and completely dominated the vast interior space. Shadows played over its length, making it seem to move, to shift, to beckon.

Zia stepped to the side wall, opened a metal box, and snapped on the overhead lights.

Seen in the glaring illumination, the craft became transformed. One moment a mythical seaborne beast. The next . . . The boat was a complete and utter wreck.

The yacht had once probably been someone's dream. Or trophy. Now it rested on a series of padded plywood supports, exposing a hull blanketed by years of barnacles and rotting seaweed. In some places the growth was two or even three shells deep. The stench of rotting fish was fierce.

But that was not what held Noah fast.

The hull was ripped open in several places—great gaping wounds almost a foot wide, most of them near or below the waterline. The fiberglass was breached outward, shaped like rancid flowers.

Noah asked, "What happened?"

"Shotgun blasts. From the damage, we're thinking sawed-off twelve gauge." Zia was almost matter-of-fact. A seasoned detective surveying just another crime scene. He pulled a notebook from his back pocket. "Here's what we know. Boat is an Azimut 84, purchased new sixteen years ago by its former owner, one Dino Vicenza, late of Santa Barbara. Gentleman died from natural causes last week. Survived by two daughters and grandkids."

Amos remained a few paces farther away, surveying the scene from a safe distance. "You're certain the man's death was by natural causes? I'm only asking because we're looking at acts of serious violence here."

"Yes, Amos. I'm sure. The gent was a hundred and two."

"You're telling me this guy bought a new boat when he was eighty-six?"

"What, you think you lose all interest in life just because you're old?"

"We're talking about a boat, not life."

Zia shot Noah an exasperated look. "You see what I have to put up with?"

Noah said again, "Tell me what happened."

"What we know came from his live-in carer." Zia flipped a page. "Jenna Greaves, age twenty-nine, gives a Miramar home address. Specializes in late-stage home care. Works all over the place. Or she did. Ms. Greaves became employed by Dino Vicenza nineteen months ago. When the old man was up to it, Ms. Greaves drove him to the Santa Barbara harbor, wheeled his chair out to the boat. She gained her pilot's license, apparently paid for by Vicenza. She took him on short cruises, nothing much. Out to the Channel Islands, tour up the coast a ways. Two weeks back, he sold the boat to his attorney, Sol Feinnes."

Amos said, "I know that name."

"Local guy. Born and raised in San Lu. I've come up against him a couple of times in court. Straight shooter. He doesn't handle much criminal. He's okay, for a guy who walks the wrong side of the legal line."

Amos said, "So Feinnes bought the boat . . ."

"Vicenza owned a dockage off Shell Beach. Had it since the early seventies. They don't sell them anymore. Worth a small fortune now. Last week, Ms. Greaves brought the boat up the coast. The old man had apparently entered into serious decline. She was clearing the decks, so to speak." Zia pointed to the nearest breach in the hull. "The attack happened two nights later. Problem is, the new owner hadn't bothered with some of the minor details of boat ownership."

Amos nodded. "No insurance."

"There you go. Ain't it a shame when bad things happen to defense attorneys? I cried real tears."

"So the boat is here . . ."

"Declared a total loss. Slated for the next police auction, which is in two days." Zia started for the stern ladder. "Want to have a look inside? I got to warn you, it only gets worse."

Noah followed Zia up the ladder, wondering why Amos had brought him to survey such tragic wreckage. Amos remained on the tarmac, observing them from below. When Zia climbed over the stern railing, he called down, "You coming?"

"I'm fine here."

"We're twelve miles from the Pacific, bro. No chance of seasickness."

"You're not even close to being funny."

Zia winked at Noah. "Suit yourself."

The rear deck faced three partial floors. The control system was duplicated: one in a pilot's cabin on the middle deck, the other on a flying bridge high as a seagoing tower.

Both sets of controls were smashed beyond repair.

Zia led Noah across the trashed outer living area and up the main steps. He gave Noah a few minutes to survey the demolished flying bridge. Then they descended what was left of the internal staircase and entered the main parlor. The floor was shattered in several places, and all the windows were smashed. The floor was ribbed with cracks and fissures that ran the entire length of what once had been a very elegant chamber. Around the edges were downward-aimed holes that exposed both the bilges and the warehouse. Zia pointed at one corner of a fuel tank anchored to the lower hull and said, "Good thing they directed their firepower outwards. Else we'd be hunting the seabed for scraps the size of kitty litter."

The secondary control system was placed inside an air-conditioned cabin, there for use in inclement weather. All four screens were smashed. Only one window remained intact. The white-leather seats were ripped open. Steering wheel shattered. Ditto for the gauges, engine controls, even the compass.

"Ax, best we can figure." Zia pointed to the stairs leading

into the main cabin, then glanced back. "Look who found his courage."

Amos pretended not to hear him. "Somebody was sure upset over something."

Zia started down. "It gets worse."

The dining area, kitchen, corridor leading to the two master suites . . .

Wreckage.

"Forensics did a quick and dirty. No reason to do more. Nobody on board. Nothing the caregiver or new owner could identify as missing. Surviving family has shown no, repeat no, interest in even checking it out."

Amos asked, "You think they had a hand in this?"

"Somebody sure carried a grudge." Zia kicked at the rubble. "Where was I?"

"Forensics," Noah replied.

"Right. We're calling it at least two perps, one strong enough to do this number with their ax. Then they tossed in a pair of compression grenades. Took out these interior walls, cracked the flooring, demolished the kitchen and the main bedroom and bath. All the windows. Boom. Probably assumed that would be enough to breach the hull. But this lady, I'm telling you, it was built *strong*. Which is when they brought out the shotgun. Bing bada-bong, then we think they motored away in their own launch."

Amos asked, "Witnesses?"

"Nada. First alert came from the Beach Patrol. Boat was resting in eight feet of water. . . ."

Zia's voice gradually faded into the background. Noah still heard him. But mostly he was now focused on . . .

The wreckage was massive. A gritty waterline stained the furniture and walls. Even so, the longer he surveyed the craft, the more certain he became.

When he looked up, he discovered both men were watching him. He declared, "I'm pretty sure I can repair this."

Amos said, "Told you."

Zia said, "You want, you can probably buy this for scrap. That's the official estimate. Might have a couple of local yards bidding for parts. Engines have less than a thousand hours on them. They can be cleaned up. The rest . . ." He waved a hand at the damage. "I had a word with the auction-eer. Nobody else has registered an interest."

Noah walked forward, taking in the two ruined master cabins. Shattered baths. So much rage. So much futile fury.

But now he was seeing something else. Standing there in the entry to what once had been a magnificent bedroom suite. Looking inward more than out. Seeing what it might mean. Take this ruined craft, rebuild it.

Try to do the same for his own life.

CHAPTER 3

Eight years earlier

The bulky envelope had arrived four days ago. Jenna Greaves signed for it on her way to start another twenty-six-hour stint as a surgical nurse. She had been fully licensed for only six and a half months, and already she felt like she had been wearing the surgical blues for two lifetimes. The work was splendid, but the resident surgeon responsible for Jenna's operating theater was a louse. Jenna hated the woman, and she suspected the doctor felt the same.

She opened the envelope on her first break, assuming it was just more of the endless stream of documents she'd been dealing with since her mother's death eleven months earlier. Instead, Jenna found herself surveying a sheaf of pages that completely and utterly upended her world.

As a result, Jenna basically floated through the rest of her shift.

Afterwards she drove home, showered and slept and woke and went for her run. Returned and showered again. Made coffee. Ate breakfast. Reopened the envelope. Read the document more slowly. Taking her time. Trying to absorb.

Her desk overlooked the rear garden of the only home Jenna had ever known. Two and a half weeks earlier, she had listed it with an agent. Even with her mother's things taken by Goodwill, the house remained far too full of old shadows. Jenna entered her mother's former bedroom only to dust and vacuum. She spread the documents over her desk. She paced.

Time and again, Jenna returned to the pages. Wondering what she should do.

When the living room was creased by another sunset glow, defeated by all the mysteries and questions the documents had created, she picked up her phone and texted.

The response came lightning fast. *Finally*, was all the message said. Following that was a Zoom link.

Ten minutes later, they were face-to-face. Sort of.

The stranger, a woman her own age, said, "I know, it's a kick, right?"

"We're half sisters?"

"I prefer to think of us as twins. Only with different mothers."

Jenna took her time, inspecting this woman. The words that best described Millicent Weathers were "old before her time." Wiry black curls laced with silver threads were bound to her narrow face, like they were somehow shaped by the same frenetic energy there in her dark eyes. Defying the bruised and fragile cast to her features. Behind her, the padded handles of a wheelchair rose above her shoulders. "How did you . . ."

"Oh, I've always known. My sweet mother loved nothing more than throwing the fact of your existence in Daddy's face." Small, birdlike hands flitted about as she spoke. "Their endless quarrels punctuated my nights. Until Daddy had enough. And paid the price for his infidelity in the divorce settlement."

Jenna tasted several comments, but the one that kept surfacing was, "I grew up wishing I could know my dad."

"You didn't miss anything, believe me."

"So you lived with your mother after the divorce?"

The laugh was bitter. Swift. Frail as her limbs. "Mom couldn't take care of a parakeet, much less a nine-year-old child. A year after the divorce, she was institutionalized. I still have nightmares of my visits to that awful place."

Jenna found herself intensely drawn to this fast-talking woman. And something more. She sat there, stared into the laptop's screen, and felt a new presence filter into her life. Soft and gentle as the dusk. She fought a sudden urge to weep. "So life with our father . . ."

"He was okay, in a cold and distant sort of way. Dad is basically the same guy who fled the scene when your mother got pregnant. Ambitious, greedy, totally caught up in climbing the corporate ladder. But the two stepmoms who entered my world and then left with some of dear old Daddy's money, they were both fairly awful."

Jenna flattened the pages that were now spread out to either side of her computer. The woman's birth certificate, naming the man whose name her mother had always spoken with fury and bitter sorrow. "We were born on the same day."

"Can you believe it? Three thousand miles apart, popping into the world at basically the same minute."

Jenna turned the page, bringing up the genetic confirmation. "My mother always blamed your mom for ruining her life."

"I can only imagine. I grew up hearing my mom's version of that tune. Crazy, right."

"What is he like? I mean, really."

"Oh, Dad can be a real charmer. Magnetic. Great smile.

Big, booming voice. Strong arms. I loved crawling into his lap when I was a kid. Feeling like he could keep out the whole world." Millie had a face that was made to smile. Even when she was bitterly sad. Like now. "That was before he became another fatality in the #MeToo movement. Too many women came forward, too many accusations, too many voices that wouldn't be silenced by payouts and confidentiality clauses. He was forced to take early retirement. The civil cases basically wiped him out. Now he's living in a fifties-and-up Tampa Bay community. Licking his wounds. Looking for a way to get back in the corporate game. Desperate. Broke." A pause, then, "Okay if we stop talking about Daddy?"

"Of course. Sorry."

"For what?" As Millie waved it aside, Jenna caught sight of dark, coin-size bruises tracking their way up the inside of a too-thin arm. "How do you like living in Miramar?"

"It's the only home I've ever known. I like it here. A lot." It was then Jenna realized this stranger who was fast becoming a friend struggled not to weep. "Millie, what's wrong?"

"Everything." She angrily swiped at her face. "I promised I wouldn't do this. Trademark of my family. Breaking promises."

"Millie . . ."

"I'm dying. I've been a diabetic ever since I can remember. The doctors have tried to write me off four times before. But this one is different. I know it, the docs know it, the nurses treat every appointment like they're all saying goodbye. Basically my heart isn't in it anymore. Bad joke."

Jenna found herself wanting to cry. Which, of course, was ridiculous. Feeling sorry for a woman she had met only ten minutes earlier. Even so, her voice sounded choked. "I'm so sorry."

"I'm lonely and I'm scared and I need a friend for the end." Two more swift swipes. "If that sounds like I'm begging, tough."

"No man in your life?"

"Men. Huh. What about you?"

Jenna loved the bond. The sense that here before her was a fragment that came close to making her life whole. "Men. Huh."

Millie took a big breath. Became the other woman. The determined fighter who had defied the medical world for years. Clinging on to a life that had clearly never treated her well. "It's crazy, I know. You've got a job you probably love. Forget I asked. I'll just—"

"I'll do it."

Millie pierced the distance with the look she gave Jenna. "I can pay. My mom's family left me a trust. Not big, but enough." When Jenna did not respond, Millie began her matter-of-fact farewell. "Look. I've already made arrangements with an in-house hospice nursing—"

"I said I'll do it, and I will." There was a weightless moment, knowing her monster of a ward doc would never in a million years grant her leave. Which meant quitting a job she had struggled and strived and gone into major debt to obtain. "What do we do? I mean, if you're that sick . . ."

"I am." Millie pulled an invisible cord. "This train is leaving the station."

"So you're living in—"

"I've rented a condo in Cape Canaveral. Bird's-eye view of rockets heading into the great unknown. Hoping they'll point me in the right direction."

Jenna saw the tears captured by Millie's lashes. The relief that tightened the woman's face and voice both. "Can you give me a few days to wrap things up here?"

"Are you kidding?" The woman's laugh was fractured. But still. "I've hung on this long. I can do a few days standing on my head. Joke."

"A terrible one."

"Hey, give the girl a hand for trying." Another of those looks. Borderline desperate. "This is real?"

"Real as it gets." Jenna promised to call the next morning Florida-time, then cut the connection. Sitting there. Watching her reflection in the dark screen. Breathing in and out. Wondering at how easy it had been to change her life's direction.

Hoping she had not lost her way in the process.

Millie clung to life for another seven months.

Long enough, in fact, for Jenna's own life to take a new and utterly unexpected course.

Millie remained cynical, bitter, caustic, and funny right to the very end. By that time, they were truly sisters. Petty and peevish one day, the next sharing dreams and all the many absent days.

With Millie's urging, Jenna enrolled in the University of St. Augustine's school of nursing and started online courses for her master's degree.

More important still, she found a calling.

Jenna was going to be nurse to end-of-life patients.

She couldn't say for certain, of course, not until she had gone through her first final act. But by the time Millie took her place in the checkout line—Millie's term, not hers—Jenna was fairly certain this was her way forward.

By then they had both endured three dry runs—again, Millie's term. Those nights had turned endless and it looked like the sunrise belonged to someone else. But Millie pulled through, and recovered to some extent, and life went on.

Sort of. In the process, Jenna had gained firsthand experience in the act of letting go. Not fighting for a recovery they both knew would never be real. Which meant accepting that her responsibilities were different from most nursing lessons she had been taught up to that point. Her job, basically, was to be the last and final anchor, the assurance that neither the pain nor the loneliness would ever grow too intense. That her beloved, dear, sweet, infuriating first patient indeed had a friend to the end.

Jenna tried to thank her newfound sister for her new life's course. Once.

The conversation did not go well.

Millie didn't even let Jenna finish. "So what you're saying is, you're glad I'm dying."

Jenna had waited for an afternoon when Millie was strong enough to indulge in her last remaining favorite pastime. The rented condo was a four-hundred-yard walk to the Canaveral port, a massive manmade harbor designed to hold three distinct sections. The private-boat marina stood next to a mile-long dockage for cruise ships. And beyond that, utterly distinct from those two, was the super-secret naval base for nuclear subs.

Millie was happiest here. Especially on days like this, when Jenna pushed her wheelchair along the quayside and they waited for another rocket launch. On such days, the Canaveral highways and marinas were blocked to outside traffic. Which meant the marina held a locals-only festival air. But that day, half an hour before take-off, the launch was scrubbed. Jenna could tell Millie was tiring, so she started back to the condo and thanked her sister. Or tried to.

Jenna was so upset by Millie's response she waited until they were in the condo's elevator to say, "That was actually all you heard? Really?"

"Hey, it's what you said."

"Was not."

"Was too. I was paying careful attention."

The doors slid open, and Jenna pushed the chair along the interior hallway. "I was the one talking. And the talkie says, you heard what you wanted and not one word more."

"Okay, I'm pretty sure 'talkie' isn't a word."

She unlocked the door, entered the bedroom, and maneuvered the chair up to the rented hospital bed. Helped her sister shift over. "You're impossible. And that's definitely a word."

"So leave, why don't you."

"That's your job. Anyway, the talkie signed on for the long haul."

Millie watched Jenna prepare the afternoon syringe. "Not so long."

"I should be so lucky."

That basically froze them both.

Jenna said, "That came out totally wrong."

"Was that an apology?"

Jenna searched for a vein that was not already bruised with previous puncture marks. "Definitely not."

"Because if it was, I'd class that as the totally lamest apology ever."

Jenna pressed the syringe home. "You are purely awful."

"Bad syntax. Again." Millie sighed a welcome to the relief. "So what you're saying is, next time I should go ahead and kick the old bucket."

"Don't you dare." She extracted the needle. Disposed of it in the plastic hazardous-waste pail. "Who am I supposed to be angry with after you're gone?" She stripped off her gloves. Swallowed hard. Added, "Who am I supposed to love?"

But Millie was already asleep.

* * *

Their final ten days together, Millie grew too weak and fragile to leave her bed. This final admission of defeat cost them both more than either expected, despite how Jenna had spent months preparing for this day. Knowing Millie would hate it worse than anything. Fight it hard as she could. And be defeated just the same.

When it was time, Jenna prepared just another dose of the ever-stronger pain meds. When Millie finally stopped her bitter venting and fell asleep, Jenna went to work.

Thankfully, Millie's sleep had grown far deeper and longer. No surprise, given the current dosage of her meds. Which was good in a way, because Jenna made ten kinds of racket.

She swung the hospital bed around, creasing the bedroom's floorboards in the process. Then she repositioned all the room's other furniture. This was followed by dragging in a stepladder, which she then fell off. Twice.

Her plan was simple enough. She was going to bring the one most precious fragment of the world, the part Millie found hardest to give up, inside Millie's room.

When Millie finally woke, all the preparations were completed. Jenna was seated in her customary position, between the bed and the door leading to the other rooms. Not actually preening, but close.

"Sit me up."

Jenna used the controls to raise Millie's head. The bed now fronted the sliding glass doors. Beyond the balcony railing, a massive cruise ship trundled out of port. Heading into the deep Atlantic waters. Caribbean islands, the Keys, the Gulf, Mexico, South America, all the places Millie would never visit. Except for the photographs that now rimmed her perch. Dozens and dozens of pictures. Boats and islands and mystically beautiful harbors. All of them plastered to her walls and the ceiling overhead.

Millie waited until the white cruise ship had vanished from view, then said, "I knew it would never happen. Not to me. Not in this life."

Jenna found no need to pretend or object. "I envy you that. Having big dreams."

"You never wanted the impossible?"

"Not like you. I never had a dream so potent I was consumed with the desire. Growing up, I considered moving from day to day and staying intact accomplishment enough." She watched as Millie focused on the two-page catalog directly overhead, her all-time favorite yacht, a seventy-two-foot live-in Bertrand. "Listening to you talk about your boats, seeing how you loved them, it makes my life seem small."

"My dreams of cruising the open waters have seen me through some bad times." Millie went quiet, then, "I always saw it as the other me. The healthy me. The one who could make the dreams real."

"The other you. I like that."

Millie turned her head without lifting it from the pillow. "How much?"

"How much what?"

"Pay attention, sport. This is important. How much do you like the idea?"

"A lot, until you started getting snippy," Jenna replied.

"Now, not so much."

This time, Millie did not come back with a semi-acrid retort. Instead, she offered Jenna the same tight and frantically electric look she had last revealed during their first-ever Zoom.

Then she asked, "Will you do it for me?"

Jenna had no idea how to respond.

Millie seemed to approve of Jenna's silence. She went back to examining the yacht overhead. "You need this. Almost as much as I want it. Consider it my last and final bequest."

"That's a big ask and you know it. Huge."

"Who else could I possibly trust with my lifelong dream?"

"Except your twin sister. The one with a different mom."

"Two halves make a whole." Millie closed her eyes. "I'm hereby bequeathing you my pretend boat. Your job is to make it real. Go somewhere really, really nice."

They never mentioned it again.

Four days later, Millie started going absent.

Jenna's focus in her master's studies was end-of-life care, and she had come across numerous firsthand accounts of such times. Millie wasn't asleep, nor was she actually present. Most specialists had their own way of describing such periods. The term Jenna preferred came from her favorite professor, who described it as, "Elvis is looking for the exit."

This period proved especially important for them both. Millie had spent her entire life fighting. Now, however, she was grimly tasked with learning how to let go.

Jenna came fully to terms with what she knew now was her career path. She observed. She noted. She cataloged. She fit what she was witnessing inside the texts and lectures framing her university course. She made all the required steps and in the process saw herself becoming comfortable with what in truth was just another line of nursing. Her job was different, of course. Hospital care, especially surgery, was all about repairing. Saving the life. Rebuilding the body. Here, in her new field, it all came down to helping the patient let go.

But still.

At some core level, for Jenna the nurse, it was very much the same. Doing her best by the patient, keeping them comfortable. Being the steadfast and professional caregiver. Doing what was required.

Millie had several online groups, all of them focused on

final days and preparing the patient and family for the departure. Jenna was gratified to discover she remained both calm and dry-eyed when she informed the groups that her sister was in full departure mode.

Their response was a pure astonishment.

Within hours, Jenna was offered three new live-in opportunities—faster than she was willing or able to accept. But clearly the need for her services was both real and urgent. In the end, though, she decided to hit the pause button. Give herself a break. Then decide.

Every day led to new discoveries. There was the mundane, such as taking care of Millie's basic needs. This proved, well, nothing really. Jenna did what was required with a matter-of-fact distance that surprised her.

Then there were the other elements. Such as how their bond deepened into a love so intense Jenna feared she would be struck dumb by the loss.

The final day proved relatively smooth and straightforward. The times when Millie was absent had grown to dominate their shared world. But in the hour before dawn, Millie came to full wakefulness. Such times were very brief now. And more precious as a result. "Will you do something for me?"

Jenna pulled her chair in closer. Reached for her hand. "Anything."

"Take my ashes to Miramar Bay."

Jenna leaned over, not in sorrow, simply so she could rest her face on the thin arm, so she could kiss the skin with its spackle of bruises. "All right."

"It would be nice to think maybe some part of me could have what you said."

"A second chance. The myth of my hometown."

"There you go."

Jenna straightened so she could caress her sister's cheek. Share a final openhearted look. And wait.

Millie closed her eyes. Her breathing was slight, a feather's push. A long pause. Another tiny breath. Then she whispered, "Here goes nothing. Bad joke."

She was gone.

CHAPTER 4

Today

In the end, Jenna decided not to attend the police auction.

Few events had shattered her world like hearing that her beloved boat, the one promised to her by the late great Dino Vicenza, had been sunk.

Sol Feinnes, the attorney responsible for her mother's estate, now managed all contracts between Jenna and her patients. Sol had introduced her to Dino, and all but begged her to take the assignment. A first. Sol had handled Dino's affairs for almost three decades, and counted the old man as a true friend.

Dino had been sharp and cautious to the end. A hundred and two years old. His body an ancient wreck. But his mind—Jenna had come to genuinely love that man's intelligence and wit.

Dino had shown a bitter humor at how his children and grandkids chomped at the bit, eager to divide the spoils of Dino's long life. The last person he had allowed into his world, his final good friend, was Jenna. And she in turn had genuinely cared for the old scoundrel.

Dino had promised her the boat.

His family would have battled for years over any such gift, however. So Dino had sold it to Sol.

For a dollar.

Sol in turn had entered into a secret handshake deal with Jenna. Sell it to her for the same amount. A dollar. A year or so in the future. After the dust had settled and the family and their attorneys were no longer clustered like vultures, hungrily surveying the carcass of Dino's possessions. In the meanwhile, the boat was hers to use whenever, wherever.

She tried not to hate the family, that greedy, impatient mob. Dino had been right to bar them from his final days. But of course this only added to the loathing and distrust they already felt toward Jenna. Especially after they learned she had been named co-executor of the old man's estate. Not to mention how Jenna had been specifically instructed to remain in Dino's home until the estate was officially cleared by the courts. If Jenna had known the hassles this would add to her life, she might have refused Dino's final request. But Dino had begged for her help. It had been hard for the old man to beg, and impossible for Jenna to refuse.

And then there was the other reason why she had accepted.

The money.

As in, two thousand bucks a day.

To simply sit in the old man's empty home, keeping watch. Refusing to let the grandchildren pass through the front gates while the legal dust settled. Why this had been so important to the recently departed, Jenna had no idea.

By this point, the family had hired their own lawyers. They were spoiling for a fight. Looking for an enemy.

Never come between the patient and her family. That was Jenna's rule number one. And two. And three.

Still. Two thousand dollars a day.

Sol Feinnes had proven good as his word, keeping the family and their attorneys at arm's length. Private security was stationed outside the gates twenty-four/seven. The children responded in a typically petty fashion, hiring their own security, stationing them on the street, hassling the cleaner and Jenna's grocery deliveries.

Two evenings ago, Sol had called to report the probate would take longer than expected. The children had gone to court, demanding entry to Dino's home. Twice. This time, the judge had granted them permission, so long as nothing was removed. Which meant Jenna's lonely days were at an end.

Jenna enjoyed a final evening in the empty house, taking her last dinner as usual on the rear veranda. Dino's home sat on a steep-sided hill overlooking Santa Barbara's harbor and the glistening Pacific. Years of neglect and hard winter storms had taken their toll. Nothing had been done to the place in over twenty years. None of the walls were truly straight. Virtually all the tiled floors were cracked, the grout yellowed, the paint water-stained. Dino could have cared less.

Jenna was beyond ready when Chuck, the day security guy, walked up the drive and climbed the front stairs. She had the door open, her two cases positioned just inside the door. "Good morning."

Chuck was like a lot of the security guys she had known, charged with steroids and pumped from spending idle hours in the weight room. "Looks like this is your coming-out day."

"Not a moment too soon."

Chuck had not been farther than this top step. Again, Jenna following Dino's orders. He pretended to inspect the vast foyer, the stained red-silk wallpaper, the parquet floors, the chandeliers parading into the home. "Looks like the perfect hangout for ghosts."

Jenna's response was cut off by spotting the eight people marching up the drive. "Here comes trouble."

"If you want some more time, I can hold them off." Chuck bunched his shoulders like a boxer ready for round one. "Taking out the trash is what makes this job worthwhile."

"There she is!" Laura, Dino's younger daughter, was a professionally skinny woman with a dyed-blond helmet for hair. She waved a sheaf of papers as she stomped up the drive. "Throw her out on the street where she belongs!"

"Not happening," Chuck replied.

Laura was followed by her older sister, Eloise, a stern-jawed woman leaning on a cane. "That so-called nurse is a menace!"

Laura climbed the stairs, still waving her papers. Chuck stepped forward.

"Get out of my way, you!"

"We were just leaving," Jenna said.

The older sister had a piercing, shrill voice. "Not until you search her bags!"

Chuck remained a human wall between them and the entrance. "Think again."

Willifred, Eloise's son, matched his mother's ire as he shouted at their own guards and pointed at Chuck, "Remove this filth!"

"The house is *ours*," his mother yelled. "And that includes everything inside." The cane waggled in Jenna's direction. "Make sure she hasn't secreted jewels on her person!"

"This is nuts," Chuck said.

"No, it's okay." Jenna set her two cases on the front stoop, then moved forward, lifting her arms. "Search away."

The family's security included a hard-faced woman who had the decency to whisper "Sorry" as she gave Jenna a quick but professional pat-down. Her male counterpart slipped on vinyl gloves and opened her cases. "She's clean."

"Get out, the pair of you." The grandson stepped through the front door, triumphant. "Coming, Mother?"

Chuck shut and lifted her two cases, then led her down the drive. He didn't speak until he had set Jenna's belongings in the trunk of her Honda SUV. "Let's hope the resident ghosts include some really hungry vampires."

As Jenna passed Santa Barbara's final exit, she was struck by waves of fatigue. The assault was strong as the Pacific was now lost beyond the western hills. Ending a case always resulted in such events. In fact, Jenna had been surprised the comedown had not appeared earlier. When her solitary days in Dino's home remained undisturbed, she had wondered if maybe she had finally outgrown the horrid hours, the wasting illness that had no name.

The nineteen months she had spent as Dino's companion was almost three times longer than any case she had handled before. When his end finally came, it had been sudden and relatively painless—a heart attack while Dino was asleep. As a way to bow out, this one was close to Jenna's top of the list.

Jenna had heard other hospice and in-house carers speak of the weight of such passages. For herself, each experience proved as tough as the first, a bone-deep fatigue that was as close as Jenna ever came to deep depression. She had read somewhere that Winston Churchill used to describe such hours as his black dog. Times like this, Jenna knew exactly what he meant.

Which was why, two hours later, Jenna took the San Luis Obispo exit, circled around the city, and took the county road north toward Miramar.

The last thing she needed at this point was to attend the police auction and view the wreckage of her and Millie's dream.

In the years since Millie's passage, owning a boat and traveling the open waters had become her dream as well. There was no logic to how her own life had absorbed Millie's yearning. Only that she felt enriched by claiming a dream bigger than any she had known before.

Her phone chimed three times on the drive north, all from Sol Feinnes. She had no interest in reliving the morning's confrontation. Nor did she want to hear the lawyer apologize yet again for not having insured the vessel. Sol had simply served as go-between. Protected her from the family's ire and suspicions. There was no reason for him to have rushed through the process of registering and insuring Dino's boat. If anyone was to blame, it was Jenna. The boat had been hers in all but name.

Sol Feinnes called twice the next day, and once more the day after. Then it was the weekend, which granted her ample excuse not to return the lawyer's calls. It was good to be home. Her haven from the world was a small apartment on an inland rise that had escaped the previous year's fires. Jenna had not even heard about Miramar's Christmas being threatened by wildfires until the end of January. Whenever she tended a patient, the world gradually faded away. Which was why she so appreciated and even liked the San Lu attorney, who looked after so much when she was gone.

Monday morning, she breakfasted, then drove into town and took a long walk along the coastal path. When she was ready, she phoned Sol's office. His secretary had obviously been alerted, because Jenna was put straight through. Sol greeted her with, "I have court. Can we be brief?"

"Of course."

"You have two requests from new patients and their families."

"Not yet."

Sol did not argue. "Can I have some idea how long before you'll be ready to take on another patient?"

Jenna had been pondering the same question. Normally a week off was more than enough to recover, restore, ready herself for the next assignment. This time was different. Why, she had no idea. "I may take a few weeks."

"The families will be very sorry to hear that, Jenna."

"Can't be helped."

"You'll let me know if you change your mind?"

"Of course."

"Do you want to hear the latest regarding the Vicenza clan?"

"Definitely not."

"You're still co-executor, so you'll need to come in and attend the hearing of Dino's will. He left specific instructions regarding several issues which must be completed prior to that. But in the meantime I have a number of documents which require your signature." The sound of pages being flipped, then, "Wednesday afternoon at three?"

She made a note. "See you then."

"Jenna, wait." When she did not respond, he asked, "Are you still there?"

She felt a rising dread over what was coming next. "Sol . . ."

"The boat didn't go to salvagers as I feared. Do you know Amos Prior?"

"The name . . ."

"Local sheriff. Good man, by all accounts. His half brother bought it. His name is . . . hang on . . ."

"Sol, I don't need to be hearing—"

"Noah Hearst. And yes, I need to tell you because he's going to contact you."

"Me? Why?"

"Because he wants to buy the mooring."

"Wait. You told me the boat was a wreck."

Sol went quiet. "It was. Yes, a total loss."

"You're not making sense."

"Here's what I know. Noah Hearst was a Hollywood set

designer. Built everything from interiors to mock cities for film projects. One of the best, by all accounts. I've checked. The man apparently got sideswiped by his former partners. Lost his company in the process. So yes, the boat is a total write-off. But apparently Hearst intends to try to put it back together. It's a massive project. A couple of local salvage specialists I've spoken with think the guy is nuts." Sol gave that a moment, then added, "I can handle this if you want."

She was tempted. But something tugged her forward. A crazy desire to meet the man who was going to try to rebuild what was left of shattered dreams. "No, go ahead and give him my number."

CHAPTER 5

Jenna lasted another week.

She spent seven days trying to convince herself how crazy it seemed, going to meet this Noah Hearst. Insane to see what he might be doing to her boat. Because that was how she still saw it. Millie's dream come true, the one Jenna had claimed as her own. Now denied them both.

Crazy.

Noah had seemed pleasant enough. He had phoned and thanked her for the chance to speak. When she asked how things were going, Noah described the multiple problems he had faced, transporting the huge vessel seventy miles north and resettling it in its wooden cradle. Thankfully, there was a vast open-sided structure near where he was renting, once used to store bales of hay and all the valley's farm equipment. The bow still stuck out into the sunlight, but at least all his work in the stern holds and motor rooms would be in the shade. Because it was hot, blisteringly so. . . .

Jenna had basically let him talk, mostly because she spent the time inspecting her internal state. She found it somewhat surprising how calm she felt, hearing this stranger lay claim to her boat. When Noah went quiet, she asked the key question, "Why do you want the mooring? I hear the boat is a wreck."

"It is. No question. And it all may be just a waste of time. But that's basically all I've got right now. Time."

The way he said those words, how sad he became mentioning his otherwise empty days, touched her. Which was beyond strange.

Jenna was still coming to terms with that when he went on. "Everybody I've spoken with has said how difficult it is to get a safe mooring for a boat like this. Especially one with its own private dock, connection points, the works. So just in case I'm able to make the craft float again, I'd like to go ahead and have a place to call home." He went quiet, then added, "Crazy as it sounds, I'm hoping it will give me something to aim for."

Again, touching.

She heard herself say, "It doesn't sound crazy at all."

"Sol, the attorney, didn't explain how you got ownership of the mooring."

"That's a long story."

Another pause, then, "I understand you used to skipper this craft. In better days."

"That's right."

"You're welcome to come down, have a look. But I have to warn you, what they did to her is tragic. Of course, that's the only way I could afford to buy her."

She liked that too. How he was taking it personal. How the boat was still, well, real. Even now. "I'll have to think about that. And the mooring."

Wednesday morning at nine, Jenna appeared in Sol's office and endured the good man's summary of all the papers awaiting her signature in the smaller conference room. She ignored his news about the Vicenza clan. She signed for what felt like hours. When she was done, Jenna watched him sort and file the papers and said, "The boat's new owner called. Noah somebody."

"Hearst. Noah Hearst. Yes, he told me. Noah has taken me on as attorney for his affairs."

"Thank you for not telling him how I came to own the mooring."

"It's none of his business, really." That much had proceeded as Dino Vicenza had requested. Sale of a pier and parking area and deep-water mooring, first to Sol and then her, for yet another bargain-basement price of one dollar.

"Noah said he'd invited you up."

"I haven't made up my mind. Part of me wants to leave it all in the past. But the thing is, I'd like to see for myself. You know. That the boat really is . . ."

"An utter ruin," Sol confirmed. "I wondered about that too. So I had another word with one of the Morro Bay salvage operators who lost out at the auction. He wasn't the least bit sorry not to have won the bid. You understand what that means?"

"The salvage operation would be more trouble than it's worth."

"His name is Wallace Myers. He was really after the engines, which have less than a thousand hours' running time, if the books are correct."

"They are. I saw to that personally."

"Then they could probably be flushed out, the electrics replaced, and resold. Wallace stopped bidding when the price rose above their value. Noah hired him to haul the boat up your way, which gave him a chance to study the boat a second time. According to Wallace, there really isn't much left intact."

"Noah mentioned something about renting a home with a barn."

"A farming valley outside Miramar," Sol confirmed. "Near his brother's home."

"The sheriff."

"Right. The salvage operator hired a construction winch, the kind you see lifting goods up high-rise building sites. They've resettled the boat sort of half in and half out of this open-sided barn."

Jenna decided she had heard enough. "If he asks, tell him I haven't decided about the mooring. But if I do sell, he's first on my list."

Sol accompanied her to the front lobby, shook her hand, and said, "It's probably best if you don't go. No need to see what they did to that lovely boat."

CHAPTER 6

In the end, though, Jenna couldn't stay away.

Noah's directions were clear enough. Eleven miles south of Miramar, Jenna left the San Lu highway and headed inland. The county road was ribbed and veined with old repairs. The hills closed in, and the road curved through several tight valleys whose sides were still scarred by the previous winter's fire. Through her open window, she smelled the vague hint of old ashes. Despite the day's rising heat, she shivered. Jenna was very glad indeed she had not been around to share in the town's fearful Christmas.

When she was on assignment, Jenna could go days without connection to the outside world. Weeks, in some cases. It was only now, driving along a sunlit road, that she felt a hint of what the town must have endured.

A ranch-style fencing began where the hills retreated and a broad, spoon-shaped valley opened up. A carved wooden sign by the tall gates read, THREE OAKS. She turned onto the narrow road and drove past simple country houses erected on broad stretches of grass and cottonwoods and the occasional oak tree. To her right, a tractor pulled a farm-size mower over an empty lot sprouting FOR SALE and BUILD TO SUIT signs. Beyond the flatland, the hill was crested by a dark streak, jagged and ugly, where the fire had tried to invade the lowlands. Jenna shivered again.

The road ended at what had perhaps been the original farmhouse. The old structure was rimmed by a broad, shaded porch with a trio of welcoming rockers. A late-model pickup truck was parked in the drive. Jutting above the home was a much taller structure, no doubt the barn that now held her boat.

Jenna rose slowly, uncertain whether she wanted to go any farther. Somewhere behind her, a dog barked. Otherwise the loudest sound was the hot morning breeze rustling the cottonwood trees. They whispered a country welcome, a soft invitation to settle down, ease away from all the burdens she still had not fully left behind.

Then she heard whistling.

She found herself drawn around the house, over to where the boat's bow jutted from the open-sided structure. Thankfully, most of the craft and its injuries were lost to deep shadows. Even so, Jenna felt a stab of very real pain.

She had seen enough.

Jenna started back to her car. If the guy was all that interested in paying top dollar for a mooring he would never use, he could deal with Sol.

Then she heard the man begin to sing.

The man could not carry a tune in a wheelbarrow.

Even so, he sounded, well . . .

Happy.

It was the sheer joy in his voice that drew Jenna forward. So close she could not fully ignore the gaping holes in the boat's side. Then she was inside the barn's shade and able to watch as a man wearing nothing but cutoffs and sneakers appeared on the stern deck, carrying two large plastic buckets filled with debris. He dumped the contents over the craft's opposite side and into a large metal dumpster. Then he stood there, hands on hips, and belted out the refrain's first line: "Country roads, take me home."

Awful. Just dreadful. It would have been painful if he had not sounded so . . .

Happy.

Then he noticed her standing there. And laughed. "Okay, now you know why I don't even sing in the shower."

"Noah Hearst?"

"I probably should apologize for offending your ears. You come about the jet wash?"

"I . . . No. I'm Jenna Greaves."

"Oh, wow. Now I'm really embarrassed. Hang on a second." He went belowdecks and returned slipping a T-shirt over his head. He descended a set of makeshift plywood steps and asked, "Did I forget an appointment?"

"No." She shook a rock-solid hand. Took in his strength, his graying dark blond hair, his height. His grin. Totally without guile or self-consciousness. He looked so . . .

Happy.

"It's really great you're here. I have a hundred questions, if you've got time. I should probably go shower before I launch in. Only, I've got this crew coming to jet-wash the hull. And I'm working alongside them, scraping off the barnacles. A shower would be wasted. . . ." He glanced behind her, his smile grew broader still. "And here they come now."

"Can I help?"

"Lady, that is the last thing you want to ask me today, not dressed like that." His grin was infectious. A great splitting of his tanned face. Shoving the weary lines to either side, making a mockery of the dark rings under his smoke-gray eyes. "Today is all about making a total stinking mess. We're aiming to spray, then scrape, then spray again."

When he started toward the two approaching vehicles, she fell in alongside. "What about the holes?"

"The salvage operator who brought the boat here claims his guy is the best. I've fitted a temporary seal over each spot. Wallace assures me they can aim the jet so the pressure won't strike those wounds. We'll see."

She liked the way he described them. Wounds. Liked his easy manner, the way he waved a hello to the two men stepping down from the lead truck. Liked his smile.

Jenna heard herself say, "I want to help."

"Like I said, you can't, not dressed like that." Just the same, he paused and inspected her. "You're serious."

"There must be something I can do."

"Not on the boat. We can't risk anybody being inside, in case the jet misfires and punches through my temporary pads." He hesitated, then said, "I was planning to run into town, grab sandwiches and drinks—"

"I'll do it."

"Really, Ms. Greaves, it's not—"

"The name is Jenna, and I'm on my way."

CHAPTER 7

Back in Miramar, Jenna's first stop was her apartment. She donned clothes she could throw away if necessary—ancient denim shorts and a T-shirt so faded she could no longer read the name of some defunct bar. Nikes with a missing logo. Fanny pack for her keys and wallet. She filled a cooler with ice and headed out.

She drove to her favorite juice and taco stand and ordered six meals to go. She had forgotten to ask how many were in today's crew, so she went back and ordered two extra.

Jenna told herself it was silly, how much she looked forward to returning. There was no logic to her actions, paying for meals and then heading back to help others work on a wrecked boat. One that was not hers and never would be.

But there was something about that guy, Noah Hearst. Good-natured, good-hearted, or so he seemed to her. Not to mention the fact that he looked better than fine, decked out in nothing but a pair of cutoffs. Of course, on the downside was his awful, dreadful singing. Which was why she was smiling as she passed the town's southern limits.

As Jenna turned onto the county road, a sudden memory took hold, strong as the hills closing in to either side. She was back in Santa Barbara, reliving the final days spent in Dino's company. She did not just remember. She was back there again, caring for an old man with weeks left to live.

Getting Dino in and out of transport was made infinitely smoother because of his money. A black Mercedes van had been fitted out with an electric ramp attached to the side doors. The rear seats had been replaced with a floor panel where Jenna could lock the wheelchair into position, allowing him to observe the world over her shoulder as she drove. Dino relished these brief forays into the outside world. She would watch via the rearview mirror as the massive bald head swung about, taking in the traffic and the people and the greenery. All the windows down, all the city's flavors rushing in with the wind. Just loving it.

Soon as she parked, two of the harbor attendants hustled over. Early on Dino had insisted she tip generously wherever possible, ensuring people would be eager to assist her. Together with the young men, Jenna maneuvered the chair and the three medical kits and the cooler with drinks and a packed lunch down the central pier. Out to a yacht so large it dominated the harbor.

They pushed him up the ramp and locked Dino's chair onto the rear deck. Positioning it out where the sun shone full on his mottled features. Dino loved the contrast of full sunlight and the Pacific's frigid bite. The attendants released the lines and stowed the fenders, the cushions used to protect the gunnels when the boat was moored. They watched as Jenna maneuvered the huge yacht away from the pier, out past the harbor's protective arms, into open waters.

The first time Jenna had taken control of Dino's boat, she had been absolutely terrified. The flying bridge and the yacht's main controls were tall as a four-story building.

From that position, she felt high as the birds, high as the clouds. Taking responsibility for a boat large as a fiberglass mountain. One that had cost new . . .

Seven million dollars.

Of course, that was twenty years ago. And since then a lot of Dino's high-priced extras had gone out of fashion. But the massive twin MAN diesels had less than a thousand hours on the clock. The boat's interior was dusty, since Dino refused to allow cleaners on board. And the fact that the old man wouldn't let the harbormaster scrape the lady's hull . . . Dino was a fanatic about his privacy. Same as with the house. It had taken four long months before Dino had grown to trust her. Her patience with his fanatical demand for privacy, her willingness to serve as both cook and cleaner, had been one of the reasons they had finally bonded. And brought her here. Learning how to handle one of the largest yachts moored in Santa Barbara Harbor.

That day, the last she had taken the old man into open waters, Dino had been both alert and fairly strong. So she headed west by north, out toward the nearest Channel Island.

The swells were running that day, driven by a storm south of Kauai. The offshore winds lessened the coastal chop, and the waves rushed toward them like midnight-blue mountains. Great shadows, some of them fourteen, fifteen feet high, forming like stripes cast across the entire horizon. Marching silently toward them. Lifting the vessel, sending it scooting down the other side. Showing just how small her craft truly was when faced with the ocean's vastness.

She marveled at how comfortable she felt, skippering this craft across the Pacific depths. All the myriad of controls, the three computer screens, the readings that told her about the engines and their positioning, she could read them now with the occasional glance. Occasionally she looked back and down, checking on the old man. All of it had been terrifying at first. Being in the middle of the mysterious blue world. Alone with a sick old man. Now . . .

She loved it.

Sometimes, when the gulls flew alongside the bridge and dolphins danced in the waters off her bow, when the whales rose and spouted geysers before sounding, her sister seemed intensely close. So bonded Jenna talked with her. It seemed the right thing to do. Offer a soft thanks, hoping the sensation was more than just a momentary joy. That somehow Millie had managed to bridge the divide and join them.

She held to a measured pace, crossing the twenty-two miles in about an hour and a half. For most boats, the approach that day would have been hazardous. The island's western side was rimmed by massive crashing surf. Because of the strong offshore wind, there was also no safety to the east. Kelp beds rimmed the beaches, floating green nets that could wrap around the propeller and snap it clean off. An inflatable lighter with a ten-horse kicker was suspended from the stern winches. But the prospect of maneuvering Dino onto the tiny craft, then motoring him home in a big swell was the stuff of nightmares.

Jenna positioned the craft just north of Cave Canyon, three hundred meters off the rocky Landing Cove beach. She set the autopilot to hold them in place via the GPS—one of the last improvements Dino had fitted before starting his decline. She descended the rear steps and asked her patient, "You doing okay?"

"Never better," Dino replied, and clearly meant it.

She opened the cooler for a couple of smoothies. Dino's arthritic hands took hold of the oversized plastic grips. He liked feeding himself, maintaining that small bit of independence on the good days. He pulled on the long straw, then asked, "Did you ever wonder why I named my boat *Contraband*?"

"I wonder about a lot of things," she replied. "But since you're probably the most private person I've ever met, I don't bother asking."

"Call it what it is," he replied. "I'm secretive."

She used a cloth napkin to clear his chin. "Whatever."

"I was born in 1919. The things I've seen."

Dino had made statements like that many times in the past. And then followed it up with nothing at all. Which was one of the many differences between him and other elderly patients. For them, the past was far more vivid than the present. They dwelled on moments, repeating stories, fading away in midsentence, fashioning a half-spoken litany that remained mostly behind their eyes.

For the first time ever, Dino continued. "My pop, he worked for the Mob. You ever heard of Al Capone?"

"Are you kidding me?"

"No joke. After Capone went to prison, Pop's boss took control of the Outfit. That's what the Chicago Mob was called back then. The Outfit. Paul Ricca was his name. Man scared me to death." A long pull on the straw. A long gaze at the island, the seals floating in the kelp beds, then, "I started riding shotgun for my dad when I was eleven years old. Pop drank, see. Drank all the time. Never got violent, not around me anyway. The old man just went quiet. He wanted me in the seat next to him, make sure he didn't drift off while we were crossing the ice."

"Wait . . . What?"

"That was his job in the winter. Hauling contraband whiskey across the lake. Dead of night, when the ice was thickest. We'd leave Chicago, the truck full of clothes from the city sweatshops. The Outfit controlled them, see. Take the bridge, drive to Canada. Rest up awhile. There were bunks in the harbor warehouses for drivers and spotters. Eat some meal, always southern Italian, pasta with a sauce heavy on the garlic, ninety years later, one taste and I'm straight back there, watching my old man pull on the bottle, watching them load barrels of Canadian whiskey into the truck."

They sat there, the yacht rocking in time to the incoming swell, the sound of waves crashing against the rocky shoreline, the gulls calling, the wind's quiet whisper. Then Dino continued. "Starting back across the great lake, my old man was always scared. He took it real slow at first, listening to the ice crack under the wheels, breathing in soft gasps that stank of his whiskey. Then faster and faster. A hundred and eighteen miles, from the Canada warehouse to the Chicago harbor. Lights off most of the way. Pop hunched over the wheel, leaning back now and then to pull on that bottle. Me watching him and the ice both. Holding the compass, keeping us on course. The truck's heater froze up a couple of times, him and me stopping there in the middle of nowhere to pile on extra layers of clothing we carried in a canvas sack just for those emergencies. The ice, it's never silent. Cracking and groaning and popping. Pop claimed that's why he drank, hearing the ice talk to him, saying how it wanted to open up and swallow us whole. Which was a lie. I knew it even then. He drank because that's what he was. A drunk.

"I loved those trips. Loved everything about it. The rumbling engine, the dark outside our cabin, the flashlight shining on the compass. Loved the way the ice smelled. That's what I remember clearest now. The sharp, clean smell of ice stretching out in every direction."

When he went quiet, Jenna started to ask if he needed anything, his meds, a coffee, when he abruptly continued, "One night Pop died. Right there, middle of nowhere. Heart attack. Pow. Me twelve years old, fifty miles north of Chicago, nothing but ice and darkness, totally alone. Dragging the old man across the front seat, climbing up behind the wheel, setting out."

"You drove?"

"It was either that or sit there and freeze. I was too short to see much of anything. Roped pads to my right shoe so I could reach the pedals. Sat on all the extra clothes I wasn't wearing. Yeah, I drove. Took me four and a half hours. Stopping every ten miles or so, checking the compass, heading on. Pop's corpse on the seat there next to me. When the city lights appeared up ahead, I bawled. Cried like a baby. Last time I ever shed a tear."

Dino resumed his customary silence, and soon after Jenna motored them back to Santa Barbara. He dozed on and off on the return journey, woke as she and the harbor attendants maneuvered his chair back into the van, and again as she brought him home.

It was then, after she settled him into bed, that Dino announced he was giving her the boat. Consider it a tip for a job well done, was the way he put it, before drifting off to sleep.

CHAPTER 8

When Jenna pulled up in front of the farmhouse, she parked alongside a sheriff's car and a dark four-door Crown Victoria. A deep thrumming resonated from the barn. Jenna left the food in her car and walked past a small tanker truck loaded with a jet-wash's diesel motor and bearing the logo of a Morro Bay boatyard. Two men in rubber rain gear and industrial-strength gloves operated the jet washer. Noah and another man worked with long-handled scrapers, finishing off what the jet wash failed to clear away. Behind them, a lean, dark-skinned man swept the hull with a wire-bristled push broom. He dipped the brush in a metal trough, then scrubbed with some soapy solution. The scrubbers wore shorts, gloves, rubber boots, goggles, and professional-grade face masks. All were hot, sweating, and drenched.

The stench was ferocious.

Then Noah spotted Jenna. He whistled loudly and waved a hand by his throat.

The big diesel powered down as the jet spray went to idle

and then cut off entirely. The silence felt almost as loud as the noise.

"*Finalmente!*" The heavyset Latino dropped his scraper and stomped away. "Another five minutes, I'd be looking for somebody to shoot."

The dark-skinned man stripped off his goggles and mask. "I would've never volunteered if I'd known how bad this smells."

"Old barnacles and reclaimed water." The jet-washer and his assistant stripped off their rain gear and shared a ratty towel. "It works into your pores."

"Reclaimed from what?"

"Best you don't ask."

The Latino stepped to the barn's far corner, pulled a cord, and water cascaded from a plate-size shower. He whooped and danced, causing the others to grin. He released the rope and shouted, "Noah, you need to fix the hot water faucet. It don't work."

The dark-skinned man was already on the move. "Cold sounds good to me."

Once they had all showered, they proceeded to Jenna's car and stood eating in the sun. Noah introduced the others in turn. The boatyard owner was Wallace Myers, the Latino a San Lu police officer named Zia, and the tall, lean man . . .

"Amos is your brother?"

"You thought those stories about *brujas* and *cambiantes* you heard as a kid were myth?" Zia was clearly enjoying himself. "Amos was left in the forest and raised by wolves. It's the only excuse for his foul nature."

"Don't pay Zia any mind," Amos said. "He's got a cop's twisted sense of humor."

"Oh, and you're so perfect with the logic and the humor," Zia retorted. "A man who gets seasick hearing about a Pacific storm, spending his day off working on somebody else's boat."

"Amos and I share a mother," Noah said. "Long story."

"I've always enjoyed long stories," Jenna replied.

"So tell the lady." Zia scratched his back on the barn's corner post. "Anything to keep me away from that smell."

"Another time." Noah began gathering up their trash. "I want to get this done while I'm surrounded by free help."

"Thank you for the lunch," Amos said.

As the four rose and started down the porch steps, Noah asked the boatyard guy if he was certain the engines could be repaired.

"Oh, absolutely. No question."

"We're standing fifty feet from the boat," Amos said. "You haven't even been down to inspect the motors."

"I checked them out back at the police yard," Wallace said. "They're first rate."

"For a boat that wound up sitting on the sea bottom in Shell Beach," Zia pointed out. "Last I checked, motors and water don't mix."

"Boats do sink," Wallace told him. "Even boats as big as this one."

Jenna hovered in the background as Wallace Myers described what was required. The salvager was friendly enough, a stubby man in his early fifties with hands permanently stained by grease and hard work. But something about him rubbed Jenna the wrong way. She kept one of the men between her and Wallace and listened as he explained how large craft usually sank from being poorly maintained, especially when kept in cold water. Brass fittings below the waterline were most often the culprit, getting corroded and then cracking with a hard freeze.

Noah asked, "So you're certain the motors can be restored to full health?"

"Oh, absolutely. These babies are barely broken in. I'll need to strip them down to the individual cylinder heads. Clean it all out. Check the wiring. But yeah, when I'm done this lady will sing."

"How long will it take?"

"Assuming there's no problem, the engines should be back in working order, say, two weeks tops." He jerked his stubbled chin at the craft. "Something else you might have missed. The size of those fuel tanks means this craft was fitted out for global range. Very rare."

"I have no idea what you're talking about."

"Most boats this size, they'll carry two, two and a half thousand gallons of fuel. Somewhere around a thousand miles cruising range." He started clambering back into his rubber gear. "This baby has eight tanks. They run along the base of the hull, form part of the ship's ballast. I'm guessing she holds four and a half, maybe five thousand gallons."

When Wallace and his assistant started prepping the jet wash, Jenna told Noah, "I want to help."

Zia pretended at shock and horror. "You best get out while you still can."

"Don't listen to Zia," Amos said. "Nothing makes that man happier than a reason to complain."

"My aching everything." Zia pulled on the rubber waders. "I'm thinking the owner of this here boat owes me a cruise to Hawaii. Assuming he can ever get it to float again."

"I'm happy to take you halfway," Noah replied, starting toward the barn. "And that boat is going to float just fine."

"Amos, tell the lady she's in for a hot and stinky and wet and horrible afternoon."

"Not me." Amos followed Noah across the dusty yard. "Like my wife says, I'm not hard of hearing. But I can be hard of listening."

Noah slowed so Jenna could catch up. "Amos didn't bring boots your size."

She lifted one sneaker. "These are my get-dirty-and-sweaty shoes."

"A lady after my own heart. You want to scrape or scrub?"

"I'm happy to do whatever. . . ."

That was as far as she got.

While they had been eating, the sun's position had shifted. Daylight now angled beneath the high roof and shone directly on the recently cleaned hull.

Seeing the damage so clearly was like a punch to her soul.

"Jenna? Are you . . ."

She felt herself clench down so tight she doubled over. Jenna did not weep. She probably would have, if she could find the air. She felt a spasm run through her entire body and feared she was going to be sick. Not even sprinkling Millie's ashes along the Miramar beach had left her so bereft. It wasn't seeing the boat. Not really. It was, well . . .

Everything.

Strong hands took hold of her shoulders. "What's the matter?"

She made a feeble effort to shrug off his hands, and failed. "I need a minute."

"Sure thing." Just the same, Noah gradually eased her upright. "Why don't we move back over into the shade."

"I'm so sorry."

"Hey. There's no need for that." Noah guided her slowly across the yard.

"I should go."

He drew Jenna up the back steps, letting her set the pace. "Just take it easy. No rush. You want to rest here in the rocker?"

"No, no, I . . ."

"Okay, sure. Let's get you inside." The words formed a comforting wash as he used his shoulder and pushed open the screen door. "Sorry about the mess. I'm not even close to unpacking. All I do is work on the boat, eat, and collapse."

Noah led her around an assortment of boxes and half-empty cases, through the kitchen and into the parlor. He settled onto a threadbare sofa that smelled of horses and old sweat. She wanted to protest, to flee, to be anywhere but here. Just the same, there was an odd comfort to be found, she the caregiver being gentled by a stranger.

She only realized they were not alone when she heard Noah say, "Amos, why don't you grab a pillow and blanket off my bed."

"Sure thing."

"I'm being so silly."

"No need for that either. Here you go." Noah slipped a pillow under her head and swept a blanket over her. She heard footsteps, then water running. He returned. "Okay, there's a damp cloth and a glass of water on the table. You rest, I'll come check on you in a bit, okay?"

Jenna nodded. Kept her eyes firmly shut. Beyond embarrassed. Unable to find anything that felt even remotely right to say.

She listened to footsteps retreating through the kitchen. Heard the screen door open and close.

A pair of male voices drifted away.

Soon as the diesel motor started thrumming again, Jenna rose from the sofa. It was so ridiculous, acting like this. Even so, hearing the jet wash and the sound of scraping, the image of those blast holes, it drove her across the parlor and out the front door. She skirted around the tanker truck and almost ran for her car. Unlocked the door, slipped inside, started the motor, checking the rearview mirror, desperately hoping the racket masked the sound of her pulling away.

She should never have come.

CHAPTER 9

Jenna woke at dawn and began just another day. Prepared coffee, fixed a bowl she set aside for later. Punctuating every few minutes with the same muttered litany.

"Stupid, stupid, stupid."

She felt utterly embarrassed over the spectacle she had made of herself the previous afternoon.

Not to mention furious with herself for having gone.

She had always considered herself able to manage almost any emotion. Keep it all carefully stowed away until she was alone. Safe. Staying calm despite whatever tempest might surround her. She considered it one of the few bonuses from a childhood dominated by her mother's emotional explosions.

Her mother had been bitter by nature. Almost everything failed to live up to her expectations. She was consistently disappointed by Jenna. Her rages were the talk of the neighborhood. Twice school counselors had asked if Jenna wanted to enter foster care. But she had learned early on to play the human turtle. Retreat into her shell. Hide in the shadows until her mother calmed. Or slip away and stay overnight with sympathetic neighbors. By the time she entered her teens, Jenna had known a secret sympathy for the father who had run away. Which was precisely what Jenna had done at seventeen. Graduated early and used a full ride from UC Santa Cruz to gain her nurse's degree and ticket out.

Her mother's final tirade and ensuing stroke happened six weeks before her graduation. Jenna spent the summer packing up and selling their home.

That next winter, she had found the home she had dreamed of. The wayward son of a wealthy family had inherited a manor he didn't want, high in the eastern hills. The son was an artist, as was his partner. Together they refashioned the vast structure into a series of seven apartments. Another six townhouses now filled the rambling lawns.

Jenna's apartment had splendid views in two directions. Her living room's French doors opened to a small veranda overlooking Miramar's northernmost rooftops, trees, and far in the distance a tiny wedge of Pacific blue. Her kitchen faced in the opposite direction, with a narrow balcony where she took the day's first coffee. This side fronted the parking area, ceremonial gates, the road, and beyond that a narrow municipal park. The city had acquired a strip of land too narrow to build on, put in parking for eight cars, and shaped a path that led uphill to an overlook. She and the other apartment owners took it upon themselves to clean up trash, tend the park's shrubs and flower beds, and keep watch for weekend parties that otherwise might get out of hand.

"No, no, no."

A pair of benches anchored the path's upward climb. And seated there was Noah. The man Jenna had vowed never to set eyes on again.

"I don't believe this."

Jenna stood just inside her balcony doors, angled so the drapes and the room's shadows hid her from view. She watched as a sheriff's ride pulled into an empty space next to Noah's late-model pickup. Amos, the angular black man who claimed to be Noah's brother, walked over and handed Noah a coffee.

"This is nuts."

Amos sat down, placed his hat on the bench, stretched out his legs, and said something that caused Noah to smile. Like the two of them were ready to wait all day.

For her.

Noah stood as she passed the front gates and crossed the empty road. Amos, however, merely smiled and waved his cup in Jenna's direction. A man very comfortable with his own skin.

Not his brother.

Noah did not actually dance in place. But the tight little shuffles his feet made suggested he was close to doing so.

She stopped where the road ended and the verge began, and demanded, "What are you doing here?"

"I just wanted to check and make sure you were okay."

"I'm fine."

"You certainly look fine." Amos gestured a second time with his cup. "I came along to assure you this wasn't a stalking kind of thing. And if it turned out yesterday was because of something my brother did or said, I'm also here to arrest him for a felony count of being a bad host."

"I was worried," Noah said. "If I said something . . ."

"I imagine it was something Zia did, not my brother," Amos said. "My pal means well. But that doesn't keep him from being off the wall now and then."

"No, it's not . . ." Jenna sighed, disarmed by Noah's concern and Amos being the low-key officer he probably always was. "I should never have gone out to your place."

"We liked having you there. And lunch was great." He glanced at Amos. "Did that sound lame?"

"Pretty feeble." To Jenna, "His heart's in the right place. But my brother's mind tends to lag a few paces behind."

Jenna asked, "Just out of curiosity, what were you planning on doing if I didn't come out?"

"We were still working on that," Noah replied.

She found herself genuinely touched by their evident concern. "I probably should explain," Jenna said. "But I'm not sure I want to."

"Now you sound like my daughter." Amos made a process of rising to his feet. "Why don't you let us buy you breakfast. Give you a chance to decide how much we deserve to know."

The Main Street Diner was well into its midmorning lull. She and Noah settled into the rear booth, where the wall offered shade from the rising sun and the light's reflection kept her hidden from passersby. Amos paused long enough to shake hands with the owner-chef, then walked over and said, "Sitting with her back to the wall. A lady after my own heart. Mind if I join you?"

She slid over. "Fewer surprises when you're facing the exit."

"There you go. Job like mine, I get all the surprises one man could ever need."

"Like a lady breaking down in broad daylight," Jenna said. "For no reason whatsoever."

"Oh, I'm fairly sure you had your reasons," Amos said.

"Not to mention how I fled the scene of the crime."

"No crime, no foul," Amos replied, smiling.

And just like that, they were comfortable with each other.

They ordered, sipped their coffees, watched the summer street scene, then Jenna asked, "Are you sure you can repair that boat?"

"Been asking him the same thing," Amos said. "And you didn't see inside."

"Bad?"

"Zia is pretty certain they finished off by letting off a couple of compression grenades," Amos replied.

She recalled the gaping holes where windows had once rimmed the cabin. Felt a momentary queasiness. Pressed a fist into her gut. "Back to my question."

"Certain, no. But I think yes," Noah said. "Maybe. With time. I can get the lady back to where she should be."

"Unpack that a little for us," Amos said.

Noah directed his response to Jenna. "My job until last week was designing and building film sets. Big operations will use outside contractors, especially when timing is an issue. A lot of my jobs were all about building things so they could get blown up. Over and over and over."

"I don't follow," Amos said.

"Multiple takes," Noah replied. "They shoot a scene. Tear my work apart in the process. Then I'm called to build it back. And do it fast."

Noah dipped the spoon's handle into his mug, began sketching designs on the table. "I've got to figure out ways of making things look totally wrecked, then put them back together. Fast as possible, like I said. A hundred-million-dollar production, say, will need around four months to shoot. Call it a million dollars per day. Time is a critical issue. So me and my crew, we build so we can wreck and then rebuild in a matter of hours. You get a feel for what just *looks* like utter ruin but can be quickly reconstructed."

Their meal arrived, and they paused until the plates were emptied and set aside. Then Amos said, "You were talking about a set. This is a yacht. Which means it has to float. No leaks allowed."

"Fiberglass is amazing stuff. If you know what you're doing, you can repair holes a lot bigger than what they did to that boat. I intend to reinforce every hull repair with two layers of carbon fiber. Done right, the repairs will form a seamless whole. You'll never know the hull was ever breached." Noah settled back, stared out the window, but Jenna was fairly certain all he saw was the craft. "I've done some checking. Below the waterline, the builders used something called vinyl ester resin."

"That's a good thing?" Amos asked.

"Best there is. Isophthalic resins have to be applied by hand. Which makes it too expensive for anything but the finest vessels. But once it bonds with fiberglass and carbon fiber, the stuff is hard as titanium steel."

"You hope," Amos said. "And if you get it right."

"Nobody's pushing you to do a single solitary thing more than what you've done so far," Noah pointed out.

Jenna asked, "How long will it take?"

"I should know whether Amos is right and I've made a terrible mistake in a couple of weeks. Maybe less."

"Don't you go putting words in my mouth," Amos retorted. "That's not what I said and not what I meant."

"As for the complete refit . . ." He smiled. "Depends how long I'll need to raise the cash."

The booth went quiet then. Jenna could see they both wanted to ask her what had happened, and why. But neither man spoke another word. Nor did they meet her eye. She found it oddly touching, how concerned these two strangers were for her well-being. Noah especially. She sensed he was worried that he might have had a hand in causing her to unravel.

So she started in, choosing her words carefully. Determined not to reveal any shred of truth more than was necessary to ease their minds. "You know about Dino Vicenza."

"The boat's previous owner." Amos's gaze met hers. "You were his carer."

"For nineteen months. By far the longest I've ever been with a patient." She turned to the window. Remembering. "Dino became a very close friend. Another thing I don't generally allow myself. But he was . . . special."

Noah asked, "How so?"

"Sharp to the end. Extremely observant. Very clear on who he was. And very private. The man loved his secrets. I learned early on never to ask questions about what he'd done, where he'd lived before Santa Barbara, his professional life, his personal history. A lot of my patients, the past is clearer to them than the present."

"Dino was different," Noah said.

"What Dino wanted to tell me came out naturally. Because I respected his reserve, who he was, he . . ."

"Let you in."

"I knew from the very start he was lonely. Hurting over how his family treated him. Like the guy should already be in the ground, and his refusal to just go ahead and die was keeping them from what was rightfully theirs."

"Family," Noah said. "Huh."

She glanced at the men. Amos was watching his half brother. Smiling slightly. Eyes caramel-dark and warm.

Noah had shifted forward. Leaning on his elbows. Closing the distance. Totally engaged. She met his gaze. Just for a moment. Felt the intensity. The caring concern.

She blinked. Broke the connection. "I'm sorry. Where was I?"

"Dino Vicenza," Amos said. Still focused on his brother. Still smiling. "Your late pal."

"He loved that boat. I think maybe he saw it as his last

road to freedom." She turned back to the window, smiling at the memories. "Trapped in either his bed or his chair. Never standing up again. Never doing anything on his own. But we'd carry him out there and clamp the wheels to the stern deck, and suddenly the man was alive."

"I know," Noah murmured, "just how he felt."

"He hated being a burden. Not because of me, not specifically. Dino was the most independent-minded person I'd ever met. When he couldn't do something, when he had to ask me to take over, it cut deep."

"Sounds like quite a guy," Noah said.

"Dino had his dark side. Every now and then I'd catch traces of some latent fury, then he'd get it back under control and he'd be the same old stoic gentleman who'd become my friend. Towards the end, I'd use the boat as a way of keeping him from giving in to the frustration and the despair. I knew that was how he felt, watching his last days just slip away." She found it necessary to wipe her face. "We'd check the tides and weather and wind, spend hours studying the charts. We'd decide on the day for our next outing. Which was the only reason Dino knew what day of the week it was. Counting down to the next time we were heading out."

"He loved the boat," Noah said.

"So much."

"And over time you two became very close."

"We did, yes."

"And then you come around the corner of my house," Noah said. "And there it was. All beat-up, smashed, and blasted by shotgun fire. No wonder you had a bad moment."

She met his gaze again, saw the caring, the understanding, and suddenly it was all Jenna could do not to tell him the rest. How she had been promised the craft. How it was to fulfill a dream she'd inherited from her own half sister. The urge was so intense, she had no choice but gather up her purse and slide from the booth. "I better go."

Of course they rose with her. And refused her offer to pay. And stood watching as she left.

But when she pushed through the diner's exit and stood there on the sidewalk, blinking in the light, Jenna had no idea what to do. The old man was *right there*. The sensation was so intense she was tempted to do the same as in Noah's backyard. Just fold up, release herself to the sorrow and the utter futility . . .

"Jenna, wait."

She jerked in surprise, turned to find Noah standing there. Still smiling. Only now she saw how one side of his mouth was canted slightly. As if his own unseen weights pulled the edge down. Revealing a vulnerability. And secrets all his very own. "Yes?"

"Have dinner with me. Not tonight. Well, sure, tonight if you want. But I'm still full from this meal . . ." His grin stretched wider, the canted weight even clearer now. "That is the lamest invitation for a date ever."

She found herself smiling. "Thank you," she heard herself say. "I would love that."

CHAPTER 10

Two evenings later, Jenna was seated on the bench outside her front door, basking in late-afternoon sun. Listening to birdsong. Feeling the strengthening sunset wind blow off the Pacific. Tasting the vague salty spice, even this far inland.

Defeated.

Two or three times each day, Jenna had stood by her narrow desk, phone in her hand. Getting so far as to code in Noah's number.

Now here she was, dressed and made up, hair washed and brushed until it shone. Slacks and top straight from the dry cleaner's bag, last worn so far back she couldn't even read the tag. Which said a lot about her life between gigs.

Excited.

She had been ready for almost an hour. The apartment had grown cramped, so she came out here. Enjoying a breath of evening coolness, another reason she loved the central coast. Waiting for the man she had vowed never to see again, or speak to, anything. For all the right reasons. Well, no, not exactly. All the *logical* reasons stacked up against her going out on this date.

For reasons she could not explain, going out with Noah opened the door to her years of wrong moves in the male department.

There had been two serious relationships, one her last year at university, the second while working in the hospital's surgical ward. The second had ended only when her ex had offered her a ring. Which had happened two months before Millie popped into her world. And changed the course of Jenna's life pretty much for good.

She closed her eyes, willing the past to go back inside her tight little box of bad memories. Instead, she saw the guy who claimed to love her kneel by the table in a fancy Santa Cruz restaurant, the one she had never entered again. And there in his eyes she had finally recognized that it wasn't him. It wasn't her either, not really. She simply had not been able to grow beyond the wounds and bitter rage that governed her mother's life. Not to mention the emotional distance that had protected her all those years.

Since then, she had been careful not to allow things to deepen to the point where she might have to confess how little she felt about any man.

Of course, that was why she had agreed to go out on a date with Noah Hearst. Because he was the perfect wrong guy. Recently divorced. Jobless. Living in a patched-up farmhouse. Working on a boat that would never float again.

And here he came.

Even so, she could not deny the tight flutter of excitement as he pulled through the front gates. Or how she smiled and waved a welcome. Or how the evening already sparkled. At least for her.

*   *   *

Noah had already slid from the driver's seat when Jenna slipped inside. "So much for rushing around and opening your door."

"I can step back, let you play the gentleman."

"No, it's just . . ." His smile was as nervous as his gaze. "You look very nice."

"Is it okay for tonight? I'm a little out of practice."

"Good." He shut his door. Sat there, shaking his head to the wheel. "That sounded totally awful."

"Noah."

"Why does everything sound lame even before it comes out of my mouth?"

"Do something for me." It was a practice she often used with new patients. When they were frightened and nervous and hating how this stranger was about to be put in charge of their life. Which was a terrible way to start her first date since entering into Dino's care. Nineteen months. Longer. But it was all that came to mind. "Forget being nervous. Just for a moment. Take a deep breath. Good. One more. For me." She watched him relax a trifle, then said, "So tell me the absolute worst thing that can happen tonight."

"You mean, other than you having a terrible time?"

Hearing those words, how his first concern was for her, brought a smile. "Okay, the second worst."

"We'll show up at Ryan's place and there will be this other woman there."

This was a new one. "Other, as in, a blind date?"

He nodded. Still staring out the front windshield. "Amara has a friend, she and Ryan have been dying to set me up."

"Amara?"

"Ryan is a cop. Miramar's only detective. She's in a relationship with Ethan Lange, my closest friend in Miramar. Other than Amos, of course . . ."

"You're doing fine. Go on. Ryan and Ethan are a couple. And Amara . . ."

"Amara is a neighbor and close friend. She looks after Liam when Ryan is on duty."

"Liam is . . ."

"Ryan's son. He's twelve. Liam is . . ."

She sensed Noah's nerves were easing. "Why don't you start driving, and you can tell me about Liam on the way."

He put the truck in gear. "Liam is special. Which is both good and bad."

She shifted around so she could lean against the door and take this moment to study him openly. The clothes confirmed Noah's unmarried state—clean and unironed, khakis and faded knit shirt, big hands, a pale stripe where his wedding ring had rested. For years. "Give me the bad side first."

"Liam is the quietest kid I've ever met. He can go days without speaking a word." He turned onto the road leading back into Miramar, taking it slow, winding his way through the tight curves. "Ethan has started opening him up. They're best buddies now. Which is amazing, Ryan and Amara both tear up talking about the bond between these two."

Of all the things she could imagine hearing about a boy entering the teenage years, being quiet did not register on Jenna's awful scale. "Silence is fine by me."

"I bet it is."

"What makes you say that?"

He glanced over. Nerves resurfaced. "You really want to know?"

"Yes, Noah. I'm asking a real question. I'd like a real answer."

"Your job. Taking care of people, you know . . ."

"On the way out. Right. So?"

"I can't imagine what that's like."

She actually found herself pleased to hear him say it there and then. Normally when a guy heard what her job was . . .

She decided to put it out there in stark terms. "It's not just a job, Noah. For me, this is a genuine calling. Something I hope to continue doing for the rest of my life."

He pulled up to the stop sign where her little valley road connected to the main Miramar highway. "Wow."

"Yes."

Noah showed her the evening's first smile. "I imagine your saying that to some guys leaves them playing like Elvis."

"More desperate to find the exit than my patients," she confirmed, liking how easy it was to share a smile. Especially about this. "You got that right."

His smile faded, smooth and swift as a cloud passing before the sun. "I had a calling. I lost it. Well, I guess it's better to say it was stripped away."

She nodded. Liking how he could reveal something that left him not just open, but raw. "We were talking about the son."

"The artist. Which brings us to Liam's good side. The kid is beyond gifted. He actually did some sketches that were used in a recent Christmas television special. *The Elvin Child*."

She felt a chill. "You're kidding."

"You saw it?"

"Only about a dozen times. I loved it!"

He turned back to the road. "You and Liam are going to get along just fine."

Chapter 11

Ryan's apartment was very nice. The lady detective was an excellent cook, and Noah's friend Ethan did a fine job as host. They were pleasant and welcoming, and very much in love. As they gathered at the table, Ryan announced that they had become engaged. Noah was clearly happy for them both. There was no suggestion of his being sad over his own fractured love life. Nor did they ask any uncomfortable questions about Jenna and her lack of relationship. The conversation through the first course of smoked salmon and homemade cream of horseradish and rocket salad was light and easy.

The boy, Liam, was something else entirely.

Jenna felt herself bond with Ryan's son. The sensation was intense, almost immediate, and utterly unexpected. Jenna spent the first part of the meal only partway engaged with the other adults. Mostly she focused on what was going on between herself and the boy—who did not speak. At all. Not one word from his appearance at the table, hair still slick from the wash and shirttail almost tucked in, until

Ethan prompted him to thank his mother. Apparently smoked salmon was one of Liam's all-time favorites. As was the second course of striped bass in a white-wine reduction. Liam was small for his age, which was remarkable, because he ate with a single-minded focus and cleared his plate before anyone else.

She instantly recognized the feeling she had for the boy. This bond was crucial to forging a solid relationship with her patients. Jenna did not even need to like the individual. She simply needed to find a way to connect at heart level. It happened more often than she had any right to expect. It was also one major reason why she considered this more than a job. A calling required something like this, a link far deeper and more vital than logic or even emotion.

Liam was nothing like her patients. He was so alive the air seemed to vibrate around his small, narrow frame. This intensity might have been unsettling, if it had been matched by rage. But in him, this wide-eyed silent child, there was no shred of any dark emotion.

As Ethan and Ryan cleared away the empty plates, Jenna realized what drew her so intensely. Liam shared one trait with her patients. One crucial element.

He was isolated.

Isolation was one of her patients' top enemies. Jenna always considered it her first priority, to identify what frightened a new patient most of all and meet it head-on. Breaking down the patient's barriers depended on this. Showing them she was truly there for them. For the long haul.

Liam was the same, only different.

She found herself wanting to enter into this child's world. Beyond any logical argument to the contrary. She felt connected, and wanted the boy to know. It was as simple as that.

While their hosts were busy in the kitchen and it was just the three of them at the table, Liam and Noah and herself, she said, "I understand you are a very gifted artist."

The clatter of plates being loaded into the dishwasher instantly stilled.

Liam watched her carefully. He had been doing this on and off all evening. Shooting her intense, measuring looks. Then flitting away, assuming she neither noticed nor cared.

He offered a fractional nod.

Noah said, "Liam is a sketch artist of the first order."

"What are you drawing now?" Jenna held herself as still as the boy. "Do you have a favorite subject?"

Ryan responded from the kitchen, "My son has become fascinated with the undead."

"Fascinated doesn't go far enough," Ethan said. "I get nightmares after seeing his sketches."

"I can't look at them at night," Ryan agreed.

"This from a cop who's seen more than her share of crime scenes," Ethan said.

Most of her early conversations with new patients took place in situations just like this. With loved ones hovering nervously, trying to protect and shield and do anything to keep from feeling helpless. Jenna did not ignore Ryan and Ethan so much as keep her focus entirely upon the young man. Because the longer she studied him, the more certain she became that Liam was undergoing secret changes. Things he might himself not yet fully realize.

She said, "Now that is very interesting. Have they told you what I do?"

Liam spoke. "You're a nurse."

"I suppose that's partly true. I'm a sort-of nurse."

"How can you be sort-of?"

"I only work with late-stage patients."

Ryan drifted back into view, followed by Ethan. Ryan held a spoon, Ethan a dishrag. Both made round Os with their mouths. Typical response from so many when they first heard about Jenna's calling.

But this conversation wasn't about them.

She waited.

Liam asked, "What's late stage?"

"They're dying. Real nurses help people heal and survive and get back to living their lives. These people can't. They never will. That's when I come in. To help them make that last incredible transition."

Liam asked, "You watch them die?"

"That's part of my job. Yes."

"Yuck."

"It's actually very beautiful. But you know what's disappointing?" She waited until he shook his head, then said, "I've never, not once in all these years, seen them come back again."

Liam rocked back in his seat.

"I keep watching. And hoping. You know. After. Maybe someday it'll happen."

Liam stared across the table. Gaped, really. Then . . .

He laughed.

"You're making fun of me!"

"No, really. All this time. Not one zombie."

He laughed again. "You really do that? I mean, like, it's a job?"

"I try to be a good friend during their last hard time on earth. I do my best to keep them from ever feeling lonely. Along with all the other stuff."

"And you watch them die!"

Ryan said quietly, "It's a lot more complicated than that."

His mother might as well not have spoken. Liam demanded, "What is it like?"

"I hold their hands. By this point, I know what's most special. Sometimes it's music, or poetry. I give them a last taste of what made life good. I try to make it nice. I let them know I'm there for them."

"So they'll wake up again!"

"Liam."

"Not yet. Maybe someday." She loved his laugh. Big as his gaze. A musical gift all its very own. "Of course, if they ever did wake up again, I wouldn't be an end-of-life carer anymore. I'd be . . ."

"A zombie maker!" A third laugh, the biggest of all. "This is the coolest job ever!"

Jenna glanced at his mother, took in the overbright gaze, the way she and Ethan shared a trembly smile. She asked Liam, "Will you show me your drawings?"

Chapter 12

Noah did not want the night to end.

He drove back through Miramar with all the windows down, taking it so slow he half expected Jenna to ask why he was crawling along empty streets. But when he glanced over, she leaned against the doorframe, eyes half shut, hair drifting in slow-motion waves. Watching the silent shops and the darkened side streets. He thought she might be smiling, but he could not be sure.

The evening of good wine, great food, and wonderful people had all been made even more special by Jenna. She did not charm his friends. She bonded with them. Liam had opened up in ways that clearly astonished both Ethan and Ryan. Following dessert, the two of them had shifted over to the sofa. Jenna had positioned herself at one end while Liam leaned on the armrest, turning pages in his sketchbook. The artwork that he had rarely allowed his own mother or Ethan to even glimpse. Jenna laughing and exclaiming over the ghouls and undead that had become Liam's fascination.

They were all her friends now.

There was an uncommon depth to this woman. Noah assumed it was partly due to her remarkable profession. Or calling, as she put it. The way she held herself, the depth and intensity to her gaze, the way she seemed to measure each word, these were unique elements to a woman he truly wanted to know better.

The intensity of his feelings scared him.

As they passed the town's limits, Jenna quietly declared, "I want in."

Noah put on his blinker and pulled onto the verge. Cut the motor. Swung around so he was half facing the woman and all her quiet mysteries. "You're talking about the boat."

She opened her mouth, touched the tip of her tongue to her upper lip. As if tasting a thought. But all she said was, "Yes."

He was tempted to reply that he wished she was speaking about a whole lot more. Which he was fairly certain was the wrong thing to say, driving her home on their first date. Not then, not yet. Perhaps never.

Jenna took his silence as a reason to continue. "You saw how the boat upset me."

"Which is why we're sitting here. Discussing what's the right step for you. Because the last thing I want is to make you sad."

"That might be the nicest thing I've ever heard on a first date," she said. "But in case you hadn't noticed, I'm a big girl now."

He nodded.

"And you need help. Especially with the finances."

"Desperately," he agreed.

"I've been going pretty much from one patient to the next now for eight and a half years."

"A long time."

"Not to mention how I spent the past nineteen months caring for Dino. He became a close friend. Something I don't normally allow to happen." She waved that aside. "I need a break. But I'm not the kind of person who's happy sitting around doing nothing."

"You make a strong argument."

"Oh, is that what we're doing?" Her teeth gleamed in the darkness. "I thought this was a conversation between pals."

He decided this was as good a point as any to restart the truck. Noah waited until he had pulled back onto the road to say, "You'd be welcome anytime you want to show up."

"That's not what we're talking about," Jenna said. "I want you to rely on me. The regular unpaid helper."

He did not respond. There was no way he was going to say what he was thinking. That he was filled with a sudden desire to see this develop into something more than just working together on his boat. Or how much that frightened him. How all the wrong moves and horrible endings burned his nights.

When he pulled into her drive, Noah was still looking for something to say, anything that sounded decent enough in his head to let it out. He settled on, "I wish I could have met Dino."

"He would have liked you."

"What makes you say that?"

"You're his kind of guy."

"Nearly broke," Noah suggested. "Jobless. Homeless. Crazy about boats."

"A straight shooter. Direct. Calm. And . . ."

"What?"

She opened her door. "Was that a yes?"

CHAPTER 13

Eleven days later, Jenna had almost grown accustomed to being surrounded by cops.

Zia came most days after his shift ended and worked like an angry bear for a couple of hours. He was often accompanied by two of his fellow officers from the San Lu force. They in turn started bringing their families. And dogs.

Zia's days off, he brought his two preteen sons and wife, Briana, who were almost as passionate about boats and the sea as Zia. His family claimed to love working on the kind of yacht they could never dream of affording. Trusting that Noah was right, that the boat would float. And they might one day travel the Pacific in style.

Zia just complained.

Amos was often accompanied by Aldana, his Honduran wife, and their two teenage daughters. Amos continued to insist he was totally indifferent to the entire episode. That was his favorite word for describing the days and hours he spent in Noah's company, just another episode he had to endure. His wife and daughters, however, were totally boat mad. They all enjoyed spending time with the group and clearly loved their newfound relative. Noah's gratitude for their company and help was touching.

Ethan was there almost every day after the bank closed. He was a master when it came to small and intricate work. More often than not, he brought Liam. When Ryan's schedule allowed, she came out and cooked a meal large enough for the entire crew and their families. Various people served as Ryan's assistants. Twice during those initial two weeks Ryan was accompanied by the Miramar Chief of Police, Porter Wright, and his wife, Carol.

That evening, when Sol Feinnes arrived without warning, there were seven cop cars parked in the drive and the yard and the road that ended by the farmhouse. Half a dozen kids and as many dogs raced in the field beyond the barn, chasing Frisbees and footballs. Amos and Aldana tended a fire pit, basting a side of beef with their brand of barbecue sauce. Ryan was seated on the porch with Liam on his knees by her rocker, drawing. Earlier that week he had temporarily put his ghouls aside and started doing faces. A flat rate for purchasing his portraits had been set by the mother in question. Thirty bucks. A fortune to the twelve-year-old. Even so, Liam rarely relinquished hold of a sketch. For the mother, it was a happy way of turning her son further away from the undead.

Jenna was using a newly purchased food processor to chop cabbage and carrots with a few green peppers and a hint of kale for her special coleslaw recipe. The air was rich with fragrances of roasting potatoes and meat and fresh-baked bread. She watched Sol spot her through the open kitchen window, climb the rear steps, and be halted by the sight of Liam's drawing. She dried her hands and stepped through the screen door. "This is where I ask you what you're doing here."

Sol remained bent over Liam's shoulder. "This is amazing."

Ryan asked Jenna, "Is he an unwelcome guest?"

"Ryan Eames, meet Sol Feinnes. Sol is a San Lu attorney. Ryan is a detective on the Miramar force."

"Afternoon, Officer." To Jenna, "Is there somewhere we can talk?"

They stopped by Sol's car so he could strip off his jacket and tie. Then they started down the gravel path that began where the road ended, running between the two fields, heading out to the fire-branded ridge. When they were well away from the house, Sol said, "I actually came to see Noah. He's requested my involvement in a number of issues related to his putting down roots. Apparently I'm part of his making a clean break from LA."

She searched for the right response, and decided on, "He's a good man."

"That's my impression as well." They walked on. Then, "What are you doing here, Jenna?"

Because it was Sol who asked, her attorney on all in-house care contracts, adviser on her mother's estate, her friend for over a decade, Jenna gave him the truth. Even though it left her thoroughly unsettled, speaking the words aloud for the first time. "I like him. A lot."

A sunset wind gentled its way from the west, carrying with it the day's first hint of coolness. The grass rustled and whispered, as if wanting to join in their conversation. Sol's lack of response acted like a goad at heart level. Jenna went on. "Noah has a rare quality that speaks to me. Honesty fits, but it's not enough."

"He's genuine," Sol said. "I sense that as well."

But she wasn't done. The words seemed to rise of their own accord. Carried by a force that simply would not be denied. "I've spent the past eight and a half years going from one critical care situation to the next. Dealing with families, caring for the patient's final needs, being there at the end . . ."

She liked the feel of the wind on her face, the hint of Pacific mist, the descending sun burnishing the dry valley. Sol seemed willing to walk there alongside her for as long as it took. Jenna released the midnight thoughts. The soft worries that drew out tears no one ever saw. "My work doesn't fit with anything like a normal relationship. Nine years and counting, I haven't even known a man well enough to have him break my heart."

Sol's hand drifted up, settled gently on her shoulder. Then dropped back to his side. A punctuation soft as the sun and the wind. "I understand."

"I'm not saying Noah is the one. It's just . . ."

"You want a taste of normal."

There was no reason why being understood would cause her eyes to burn so. "I'm not stopping with my patient care. I'm simply saying I'm not ready to take on a new assignment. Not yet. For the first time in what feels like forever, I need a break."

"Sure, Jenna. I get that. A job like yours . . ."

"Any job."

"What you do is not just any job. Especially when you're with a patient as long as Dino."

"Nineteen months."

"Which brings us to the point."

She took a hard breath. Decided this was as good a moment as any to draw away from the sunset confessional. She pointed them back around. "I thought you were here to see Noah."

"Actually, you were why I agreed to drive up after court today. I need Noah to sign some papers. I need you to meet me in Santa Barbara."

"No, Sol."

"Tomorrow afternoon, Jenna."

"I told you, I want nothing to do with Dino's family. They despise me. You have to handle this."

"Tomorrow is the official reading of Dino's will. You're

legally obligated, Jenna. You need to be there." When Jenna merely shook her head, his voice hardened. The courtroom lawyer coming into his own. "The will is only to be read in the presence of both executors. Dino insisted on this. Which means you and me. Together."

She kicked a loose rock. "That old man is laughing at me. Looking down. Or up. And laughing."

"My office. One o'clock." Sol knew when it was time to accept victory, and changed the subject. "Show me the boat?"

Noah met them as they approached the farmhouse, shook Sol's hand, accompanied him to the car, deposited Sol's files in the kitchen, then agreed to show him the boat.

The happy, weary, sweaty crew was washing up and shifting toward the firepit and trestle tables between the house and the boat. The barn held plenty of space for everything to be brought inside when it rained. Folding chairs were spread across the rear lawn, several clusters of families and friends. Kids were gradually shepherded toward the outside sink, where they shouted and complained as they cleaned up. Dogs were everywhere.

Sol traced his hand along a gleaming outer hull. Once the holes had been filled in, the entire structure had been coated with epoxy, then buffed until it shone like a giant pearl. "Gun to my head, I couldn't tell you where the damage was."

"That's the great thing about working with fiberglass," Noah said. "Do the repairs with care, the results can be pretty incredible."

As Sol climbed the stairs positioned by the stern deck, he said, "You've got yourself quite a crew here."

"They'll be leaving now that the interior has been cleaned up," Noah replied. "From this point on, it becomes a specialist's job."

"That's not what I mean. You and your project have become part of this community. I'm happy for you."

Noah turned and smiled at Jenna. "Me and my crazy dream."

Sol reached the top step and declared, "This is amazing."

A broad plywood platform held tools and materials for the next day's work. Jenna stepped in between the two men and shared Noah's smile.

All the damaged articles had been torn out. Remnants of the three internal floors, the kitchen and master bedroom and bath were all visible through what was left of the walls. The shattered windows and their broken aluminum frames were gone. New glass was stacked in carefully insulated sheets along the barn's north wall. Seventeen made-to-order frames were scheduled to arrive in another week.

The motors were rebuilt, the wiring an orderly array as thick as Jenna's thigh. The bilges were spotless. The two massive propellers leaned next to the glass.

"The boat looks . . ."

"Real," Jenna said.

"I was going to say in excellent shape. But real certainly works."

"Warren will test both engines tomorrow morning," Noah said. "Fitting the interior control room comes next. Electricians promised to be here tomorrow at eight. Which is why we've been pushing so hard to get done with phase one."

"He means the cleanup," Jenna said.

"I've seen enough." As Sol started back down the stairs, he said, "Truth be told, I never thought I'd be asking you this. But from what I've seen . . . When do you think you'll have this completed?"

"It'll be a good while yet. Paying the mechanics and electricians, not to mention the first set of controls, leaves me pretty much broke. Which means I'll be working in stages when I've put together the next payment." Noah stepped on the barn's hard-packed earth floor and turned to gaze at the craft. "Once I can afford to buy the wood and the special epoxy, Ethan's offered to do the floors and the walls."

Sol asked, "Epoxy?"

"All joints and seals have to flex." Noah pounded a fist on the boat's side. "It looks solid, but in a heavy sea this baby shifts. Regular sealants will crack. Floors splinter. Plumbing becomes a nightmare."

"Expensive?" Sol asked.

"You don't want to know." They started back toward the crowd. "Ethan's a master with wood. A true artist. Anything he does is going to be first rate. After that comes rebuilding the flying bridge, replacing the kitchen, and then working on the two master suites."

Jenna found herself tempted. More than that. She had to fight down a sudden urge to take the next step. Dive in. Offer a partnership. The desire was strong as hunger. It felt as though she clenched every muscle in her body just to stay silent.

Sol glanced over, studied her a moment, but all he said was, "Whatever they're cooking sure smells great."

CHAPTER 14

There was a warm finality to the meal, a sense of farewell that overshadowed the happy chatter. Zia played his role as the complaining clown. Parents chided children and ordered dogs to behave. No one paid them any mind. Jenna thought it all formed a fractured melody. These strangers were now Noah's friends.

Zia made coffee while his wife brought a trio of home-made pies from Noah's fridge, a vanilla custard and two key lime. As Zia started filling mugs and passing them around, he moaned, "My aching back."

This brought a chorus of laughter from the groups, including Zia's two kids. Amos said, "Standing around giving orders is such a pain."

"I've been doing my job and yours and three others, *cabrón.*" When the laughter died once more, he told Noah, "I'm keeping tabs of my hours. Two on the water for every one I spend cleaning up your mess. I've put in enough time for six trips to Hawaii."

"A trip to Catalina might be closer to the target," Amos replied.

Zia waited until everyone had finished their desserts and recharged their mugs, then turned his attention to Jenna. "So. This gig of yours."

Jenna had the sense all the cops and many of their wives had been waiting for this. Someone to ask questions about her work. "Yes."

Sol was seated on the long table's opposite side, down between Noah and Amos. He said, "In Jenna's case, it is a true calling."

Zia pushed his chin forward. A facial shrug. "Calling, job, whatever."

"There's a difference," Sol replied. "A big one."

"Never argue with a lawyer," Amos said. "Especially one of the good guys."

Sol went on. "Jenna specializes in situations where there isn't anyone else."

Zia asked Sol, "The lady can't answer for herself?"

"Just protecting my clients," Sol replied. "I've handled Jenna's contracts since she started down this road."

Jenna decided it was time to weigh in for herself. "Sometimes they're just alone, as in no family to speak of. Most times, though, it's more complicated."

"Families spread out over thousands of miles," Sol said. "Busy with work and children and problems of their own."

"They face issues that can't be set aside because a relative is ill," Jenna said. "It's one thing to travel in for a weekend or a week. Another to be there for as long as it takes."

"Jenna handles everything involved in caring for such people," Sol said. "Emphasis on the word *care*. Families know they can trust her to do what they can't. Jenna moves in. She's on call twenty-four/seven."

"I have help."

"Jenna hires carers for the nights, and to spell her on rare days off. But she's the one the families rely on." Sol's dark eyes sparked in the candles and torchlight. "I've heard it from countless clients. Jenna is there for her patients. Heart and soul."

"Everyone needs a friend at the end," Jenna said.

"For every new client Jenna takes on," Sol said, "I turn down ten. More."

"You never told me that."

"Why should I trouble you with all the pleadings and desperation? That's my job."

The tall grass beyond the light's perimeter rustled and rushed. Silence held the group until Zia said, "What about this last guy?"

"Dino Vicenza," Sol said. "He was altogether different. His family . . ."

"Let's not spoil the night," Jenna said.

But Zia insisted, "What about the guy's family?"

His wife said, "Zia, honey, your fangs are showing."

"I'm just saying—"

"And I'm saying, let it go. Else I'll make you go sit in the car."

Jenna could see how the group took a mental step back. Cops and their families, most of them, were used to direct questions, equally straight answers, and boundaries around what they might never uncover. But she wasn't done. She knew it with a certainty that defied logic.

"I want to tell them," she said. "About what happened."

Sol did not appear the least surprised. He asked, "Are you sure that's wise?"

"No, not at all," she replied. "But I want to just the same."

CHAPTER 15

Noah loved the evening hours, seated here on his back porch. The valley was beyond quiet. There were no streetlights, and the nearest neighbor was two hundred yards back up the valley road. On clear nights like this, the stars formed a silver wash, so bright they turned the pastures into pewter seas. The wind had died to a soft whisper, carrying enough of a chill that he and his two remaining guests had slipped into jackets. Sparsely planted cottonwoods and a few oaks marched down to the valley's far end, where they joined with gnarled olive trees. They shone in the dim light like ancient sentries.

There were only three cars still parked by the old farmhouse. Noah's pickup stood between a San Lu unmarked detective's ride and a sheriff's car. Zia's wife had left almost an hour earlier, their sons in tow. Zia and Amos were both on late duty. They rocked quietly, cradling mugs Noah kept charged, whiling away the hours before they went on patrol. Noah was tired, and with Wallace and the electricians both scheduled for the next day, his morning would be an early one. Just the same, he was grateful for the company.

Finally, Amos said, "All the things I might have expected to hear tonight, Jenna's story would never have made the list."

"I knew there had to be a connection deeper than her skippering the old man's boat," Noah agreed.

"Makes sense, though," Amos said. "One of Dino's spoiled offspring catches wind that the lady who's keeping them out of the house is about to inherit the old man's favorite possession. So they do a number on the boat."

Noah asked, "Any chance you could go after them?"

"You heard what Zia told you back before the auction. Forensics turned up nothing. Hard to get prints off a boat partially sunk in eight feet of water."

Zia, however, was thoroughly unimpressed. "You might want to stop and think. The lady, she could be scamming you."

Amos stared at his friend. "Say what?"

"I'm serious, man. She could be playing our pal big-time."

"First time we met," Amos replied, "I knew there was something seriously twisted about you."

Noah said, "I don't think that's happening here."

"You don't think," Zia scoffed. "How many good men got taken down by conniving women when the guys were thinking with something other than their brains."

Noah shook his head. "And I know that's not happening here."

"What about the lawyer?" Amos demanded. "He sat there and confirmed everything the lady told us."

"Who knows what any lawyer is really thinking."

"You're a piece of work, you know that?" Amos poked his buddy in the chest. "You're the one who suggested Noah use Sol."

"Hands off the merchandise."

"I was right there beside you, listening to your wife talk about how great Sol Feinnes was. Not to mention his newest partner."

"The lady," Zia said, nodding. "Megan Pierce."

"Best friends with your wife, didn't I hear you say that?"

"Again, another lawyer."

"Tell you what," Amos said. "Next time we want to hear from the crazy fringe element, we'll come looking for you. Until then, you best be keeping your opinions in your back pocket. Where they belong."

"I'm just saying."

"And I'm telling you, Jenna Greaves is as real as they get." Amos turned to Noah. "I like her."

"That makes two of us."

Zia rose and tossed the remnants of his mug over the railing. He jammed his hat on his head and started down the steps. "I can smell trouble on the wind."

"You'll have to excuse my friend. He doesn't know when to stop playing cop." Amos said it loud enough for the words to track Zia across the lawn.

"I'm not playing anything," Zia retorted. He slammed the car door, gunned the motor, and sprayed gravel in his departure.

Noah watched the headlights gradually become swallowed by the night. "I can't tell you what it means, being able to call this place my temporary home."

"The valley does grow on you, sure enough." Amos drained his mug and rose slowly. "What are you going to do with what Jenna told us tonight?"

Noah was fairly certain he knew the answer to that question. He had thought of little else since Jenna's surprise revelation. But he wasn't ready to shape it into words. Not just yet. And then there was the issue of who should be hearing it first. So all he said was, "I haven't decided."

Amos walked into the kitchen, rinsed out his and Zia's mugs, then returned and stood over Noah, studying his brother. Then, "Yeah, you have."

When Noah did not respond, Amos patted his shoulder and left the porch. He stopped by his ride for a long moment, a silhouette facing back toward the farmhouse. Then he climbed into the driver's seat, started the motor, and headed out. Leaving Noah alone with the night.

CHAPTER 16

Noah called just as Jenna was leaving Miramar. "I hope you understood the farewells I gave most of the crew last night did not include you."

She recalled the way Noah had walked her down the line of vehicles to her ride. How he had thanked her for sharing the events surrounding Dino and her boat. Sounding almost formal. And solemn. Like he truly valued what she had to say. The warmth and concern in his gaze and voice had calmed away her fears over having done the wrong thing. They had also gentled her into sleep. They were with her still. "I knew that. But thanks for saying it anyway." Over the car's speakers she heard the rumble of a massive engine. "What's that?"

"Warren is testing the engines. And the electricians were here on time. They woke me at six. Zia and Amos didn't leave until after midnight."

"You should take the afternoon off."

"If only."

"I'll write you a note."

"I'm pretty sure these crews don't care. They should, but they won't. Where are you now?"

"On my way to San Lu. For a meeting that might last centuries. Or at least feel that way."

"Does that mean you won't be coming by?"

She smiled over the disappointment in his voice. "Sol insists on my being there for the reading of Dino's will. I have no idea how long that will take."

"Maybe the old man left you a million bucks."

"Even if he did, I wouldn't take it. I'd only fight the family for years."

"For a million bucks, I might help you fend off a few nasty relatives."

"You don't know Dino's family," she replied. "Or their lawyers."

"So I guess you won't be telling his relatives about the progress we're making on repairing his boat."

She laughed at that. "Tempting, but no."

"Can you stop by after?"

"Again, tempting." She loved the way he asked. Like it mattered to him. A lot. "But it's probably best if I go home, open a bottle of something, and drink away the aftermath of this meeting."

"I could help. You know. With the bottle."

Her smile felt so good. So natural. "Another time."

"I have something I'd like to talk with you about."

"Can it wait?"

"Do I have to?"

"Noah . . ."

"Yes?"

"Nothing. You just sounded, I don't know . . ."

"Semi-desperate?"

"Sort of, yeah."

"I really want to see you, Jenna."

"Best if we wait. Okay?"

The engine rumbled more loudly, and a deep male voice shouted something Jenna did not need to understand. Noah said, "The guys out back have discovered I'm in here having too good a time. Got to run."

She wished him well, cut the connection, and drove south. Enjoying how he was still there with her. Even on a day like this.

The closer Jenna came to San Luis Obispo, the harder it was to hold on to good feelings of any kind. By the time she worked her way through the morning traffic and pulled into the building's parking garage, she was looking for the exit. For the first time ever, she approached Sol's office with a very real dread. There was no choice, not really. Else she would not have made the trip in the first place.

Sol's office occupied an entire floor in a modern structure built to fit into the city's old town, with stucco walls and wooden balconies and a barrel-tiled roof. The reception area was done in sunburst tones, the walls holding desert landscapes by local artists. The sitting area was comfortable, with spaces big enough to permit groups to talk unheard. Jenna thought the area suited the man, as did all of the other lawyers and associates she had met. Open, straight-talking, determined, smart. And caring.

She greeted the receptionist, refused the offer of a coffee, and wished she had never agreed to serve as executor of the old man's estate. Dying request or not. She should have washed her hands of the whole affair.

Shoulda. Woulda. Coulda.

"Jenna. Hi." Sol was dressed in navy trousers to a fancy suit, striped shirt, nice tie. He held open the little gate and ushered her back. As they started down the side corridor, he murmured, "The vultures are gathering."

She personally thought snakes was a better way to describe the clan. Every contact she'd had with Dino's family had been laced with avaricious venom. And now this. Hours trapped in Sol's largest conference room, surrounded by the clan and their lawyers, listening to them whine and moan and accuse her of everything under the sun . . .

Sol surprised her then. He gripped the handle to the conference room door, looked back at her, and whispered, "This is going to be fun."

Jenna was so worked up, she could scarcely take in what she just heard. Then she was inside. Doing her best to ignore the angry expressions, the eyes glinting with bitter greed. Eloise, Dino's older daughter, demanded, "What is *she* doing here?"

"Dino Vicenza appointed Ms. Greaves co-executor, as you well know." Sol directed Jenna into the seat to his right. "Let's see. We're still waiting on Ms. Laura Raye, correct?"

"Mom is eternally late," her son, Auburn, replied. "Let's get on with it."

"Sorry. According to the terms of Mr. Vicenza's will, that's not—" He was interrupted by a tap on the door. "And here she comes now."

The crabby woman who had confronted Jenna on Dino's front steps was dressed in the latest fashion, which might have looked fine on a younger woman. Jenna watched the family shift around, making reluctant room for Laura and her lawyer. She found herself admiring the recently departed, the way he had accepted their natures with quiet resignation. And then dismissed the lot. Refusing to allow their personalities and lifestyles to invade him at his weakest. Even if it meant he was alone at the end. Even if his only friend was a nurse there to monitor his final days.

Laura glared down the table, taking aim at Jenna. "Who is that?"

"You know full well it's Dino's nurse," her son replied.

"I am not sitting at *any* table with *that* one."

"That is certainly your right," Sol replied. His tone was deceptively calm. Even pleasant. "But according to your father's instructions, the will cannot be read without her being present."

"Settle down, Mom. Let's get this over with."

When she fumed in silence, Sol opened the slender file on the table before him and began, "We are gathered here . . ."

Jenna found it astonishingly easy to shut it all out. She shifted her gaze to the side window and could almost see Dino's smile shining there in the brilliant sunlight. Like he shared her wish to be elsewhere. Incredible how a man that old, that close to the final door, could have held on to not just his vitality but also his sense of humor. Not to mention his iron-hard refusal to divulge anything about his past. As if he was determined to do what he could and live that one day. Even if it was his last. Even if . . .

Her attention was jolted back to the room when Sol said, "There are three conditions to your receiving anything from the late Mr. Vicenza. These codicils are as follows. First, your attorneys will be barred from participating in any and all proceedings related to the disbursal—"

Laura shrilled, "*He can't do that.*"

"Actually, ma'am, your late father can do anything he wishes." Sol lifted the slender document. "His will, his rules."

"Get on with it," her son snapped.

"Second, each of Mr. Vicenza's living relatives will receive precisely the same amount, including proceeds related to the sale of his home—"

"Daddy's home is *mine!*" Eloise exclaimed.

Sol lifted his gaze. "Shall I continue?"

Willifred reached over and gripped his mother's hand. Hard.

The table remained silent. Actually, Jenna decided the better word to describe the gathering was *aghast*.

"Thank you very much." Sol went on. "The house will be sold and the proceeds divided equally. As will happen with everything else belonging to the late Mr. Vicenza. Everything to be sold. All artwork, all valuables." Sol looked up. "To that end, I have already contacted Christie's, Mr. Vicenza's dealer of choice."

This time, there was no sound.

"And finally, Ms. Jenna Greaves will today receive a gift of fifty thousand dollars cash." Sol lifted his hand to the table's unified intake of breath. As if his simple gesture was capable of shutting down the protests even before they started. And perhaps it was. "Any legal dispute arising from this or any other portion of the will, by any member of Mr. Vicenza's surviving family, results in the entire estate being donated to the Santa Barbara hospital where Mr. Vicenza received treatment."

This time, the protests formed a jagged chorus. It was hard to say who cried the loudest, the clan or their lawyers.

Sol waited them out. Jenna found herself watching the attorney more than the family. She was fairly certain Sol had to struggle not to smile. Or perhaps laugh out loud.

"I told you all along," Eloise declared, pointing at Sol. "That man is on her side."

"I am on your father's side," Sol replied. "Doing my final duty to a man I admired."

Eloise sniffed. "Whatever."

Auburn, the only offspring who had been remotely nice to Jenna, asked, "What about all the stuff my mom and aunt have taken over the years?"

"Oh, that's hilarious," Eloise retorted. "Coming from

you, who never left the place without his pockets sticking out like balloons."

"Nothing I've done compares to *your* act, borrowing his art to stick on your walls."

"For a week."

That drew a laugh from all the clan and even some of the attorneys. "Try twenty years."

Though he spoke quietly, Sol instantly halted the argument. "Whatever has already been distributed, or taken, or borrowed, now becomes the property of the current owners."

Eloise smiled at her son, Willifred. "Told you."

Auburn muttered, "That is so totally unfair."

Willifred sneered, "This from the guy who's walking away with a cool three mil. Maybe four. Who never had the time of day for the old man."

"Oh, and you were the loving grandson? Ha."

"More than you," Willifred retorted. "Better than you."

"Again. Ha."

Sol rapped the table with his knuckles. "To repeat. Any litigation or conflict arising from the sale and distribution of these assets will result in all involved parties being irrevocably cut off."

The table lapsed into a sullen silence, until Laura asked her attorney, "Can he do that?"

"These are your father's assets," the lawyer replied. "He can do whatever he likes. Within reason."

"You call this reasonable?"

Her attorney chose not to respond.

When Laura turned back to Sol, he proceeded to lay out the property sale, the agent, details related to the Christie's auction. On and on. Jenna did her best to shut it all out. She kept her gaze fastened on the hands in her lap. Every time she glanced up, she was blasted by a unified loathing. As if she was responsible for any of this mess. Jenna knew it wasn't Dino's parting bequest. Not really. His estate was worth at least thirty million, and probably a good deal more. Fifty thousand dollars was a drop in the bucket. What enraged them was her closeness. How Dino had trusted her. Not them. Never them.

She picked at a flaking cuticle and reflected on how wise the old man had been. Not allowing this pack of squabbling, greedy, grasping harpies to poison his final days.

From somewhere in the vague distance, Jenna heard Sol say, "Two representatives of the surviving family must agree to serve as official observers during the house sale and property auction."

Jenna listened to them squabble over this new responsibility, not wanting the duty, trusting no one else. She resisted the urge to glance at her watch. She had hoped to rejoin Noah, work a few hard hours in the heat, put all this nonsense behind her. But the longer this took, the less likely she'd make it back in time. Jenna could almost feel her watch's second hand beat out time's passage on her wrist.

Suddenly, without warning, she sensed Dino entering the room.

Occasionally in the first few days after a patient's passage, she experienced such moments. As if the dearly departed had popped by, or drifted in, for a final farewell. Normally a week back home was enough to fully separate her from the emotions and the passage and the person now gone. Afterward it all took a rightful place among her other memories. She had done her best by them and their clan. Their time was over. She remained among the living. Rest in peace.

This was different.

The old man seemed so close, almost like he stood beside her chair. Enjoying the squabble like he would good theater. Taking pleasure from . . . What, exactly? Seeing how they cared so much for his wealth and so little about the man himself?

No, Jenna decided. He had long known this, and simply

put it aside as one of life's unsolvable problems. Dino certainly had had his share of those. No, this was something else entirely.

She knew it was ridiculous, wondering what a former patient might be thinking, over a month since he had left it all behind. As if this was real. As if Dino was indeed urging her to pay attention, enjoy this final mystery . . .

She heard Sol say, "Your designated observers must commence with their duties this very afternoon."

The chorus of protests grew louder still.

This time, she was certain Sol could barely suppress his grin.

When the room finally quieted down, Sol went on. "They must serve as witnesses to the opening of Mr. Vicenza's secret safe."

Eloise leaned forward, said to Willifred, "I *knew* it was there."

Willifred had the ability to show a spoiled child's petulance at every comment. "*You* thought it was in the old man's boat."

"It is located, and I quote"—Sol lifted the document and read—"in the cellar, behind the central panel. Surrounded by the fuel that kept everything purring along."

Eloise demanded, "What on earth is Daddy talking about?"

"Come on, Mom," Willifred said. "His wine collection."

She sniffed. "Inside the house that *woman* was guarding. She probably cleared it all out days ago."

Sol shook his head. "Actually, Ms. Greaves's thumbprint is required, since it disarms the home's master switch. But the lady in question was not aware of the safe's existence until now. Which also requires a code Mr. Vicenza has apparently never shared with anyone. The code is 02021919, the date of his birth."

Eloise demanded, "What's in the safe?"

"I was told it contains a quantity of gold bullion. I

haven't—" Sol was halted by a tirade of voices, all demanding now to serve as observers.

Jenna leaned back, amazed at how the old man insisted on
dragging her further into this mess. In the months following
her being taken into Dino's confidence, he had insisted the
security firm recode the master alarm that controlled all the
home's locks. But this was a new one. She tried to recall him
ever mentioning a cellar safe, and came up blank.

"That is so like Pop," Laura said. "Secrets were his favorite way of avoiding human contact."

"Mom."

"Well, it's true." She pointed at Jenna. "And to have this
one involved only adds insult to injury."

"That *woman* could have figured it all out," Eloise agreed.
"Which means she's already gotten everything that's coming
to her."

"Insist on taking such opinions any further," Sol warned,
"and you receive nothing whatsoever from these proceedings."

The quarreling faded to sullen muttering between clan
members and their legal teams. Jenna sensed the old man
stepping back and turning toward the door. Actually walking toward the exit, as if he still needed a physical way out.
She felt her throat burn at his departure. Missing him and
loving him all over again.

As if in response, Dino seemed to turn back. Offer her a
merry jester's grin. Only this time, Dino was no longer the
bedridden old man whose final spark of humor and secrecy
had departed with him.

He was young. Vibrant. Handsome. Full of life and good
cheer and a certain dark edge that she had often sensed but
never truly witnessed. As if Dino felt a need to show her
who he once had been. How he still saw himself. Right to
the end.

He tipped a finger to his forehead in a mock salute and turned away.

She could actually sense the moment he departed.

Jenna agreed to drive down to Santa Barbara and return to Dino's home for the simple reason that if she didn't get it over with, she would only be forced to endure their bitter greed another day.

Sixteen of the clan members and their attorneys accompanied them back to Dino's home. She and Sol waited on the top step until all the cars had unleashed their angry mob. Jenna coded in the entry lock, stepped into the foyer, and applied her thumb to the electronic master switch. The gathering tossed what Jenna considered their standard barbs when the wall monitor chimed confirmation that alarms and locks were disarmed.

She and Sol descended the central stairs, entered the vast stone-lined wine cellar, then waited as all the others fought for space around the walls. With a nod from Sol, she knelt on the cool tiled floor. Below the wine racks ran a wainscoting made from the wooden boxes of famous vineyards. Jenna felt her way around the central segment, displaying the shields of first-growth Margaux. The panel was about four feet wide and three high.

When Sol moved up beside her, she asked, "What do I do now?"

Eloise snorted. "As if she didn't already know."

"Try pressing," Sol suggested. When nothing happened, he said, "Harder."

She did so and heard a faint click.

The entire panel came away, displaying a broad metal door with an electronic keypad at its heart.

Sol asked, "Would anyone care to code in the required numbers?"

"Oh, get on with it," Laura snapped.

"Very well." Sol counted the numbers aloud as he pushed them in: 02021919.

The door opened, revealing . . .

The gold bars gleamed ruddy yellowish-red. So many. Five drawers, set on rollers, easily four feet deep.

The bars were stacked like dominoes, each about the size of Jenna's hand. Slightly thicker than a cell phone. Each stamped with some emblem she did not recognize. Laid out and slanted so all of them were visible from where she knelt.

Sol touched her arm and rose to his feet. Waited until she joined him. Released another fraction of his smile. "As far as I can tell, there is no room for any more bars. Every space is taken. Which I think we can all assume means the lady in question has not taken anything. Can we agree?" He gave it a moment, long enough for him to step farther away and draw Jenna with him. Another. "Splendid. I suggest the sharing of these particular assets take place now, while the recipients are still gathered."

Neither of them spoke until they were standing on the front portico. Jenna asked, "Am I done?"

"We are indeed."

"I don't mean today. I mean permanently finished with that lot."

"You can't possibly tell me that wasn't at least a little bit fun." Sol was free now, and able to reveal his full grin. Stretching his face from ear to ear. He slipped on his sunglasses and started down the front steps. "I can almost hear Dino laughing."

CHAPTER 17

The next morning Jenna left her home and skirted around Miramar, heading to Noah's. She had slept well and awoken filled with a sense of calm determination. She was certain of the next steps. That is, if Noah agreed.

This day was not ruled by the logic that dominated her life. Jenna considered this a good thing. It was time to move beyond the boundaries of her careful existence.

This was not about safety. This was about something else. Something that did not fit into a neat little box of rules and doses and regimens.

When Jenna passed through the valley's gates, she followed a d-ride, a detective's unmarked car, toward the farmhouse. She knew who it was on account of how their progress was marked by the hidden lights flashing on and off and the siren causing all the valley's dogs to howl.

Noah was standing out front when Ryan pulled up. He waved to Jenna, hugged the lady cop, shook Ethan's hand, smiled broadly at Liam and ruffled his hair. Jenna hung back, wanting to speak with him alone.

But Ryan took hold of her son's hand and led him over to where Jenna stood by her car. "Go ahead, hon. Ask her."

When Liam continued to dig the toe of one sneaker into the dust, Jenna squatted down. "We're friends, right?"

Liam nodded.

"Friends can tell friends anything. That's rule one in my book."

Ryan gave her son's hand a gentle tug. Said again, "Ask her."

Liam's voice was soft as the hot morning breeze. "I want to draw you."

Ryan corrected, "Please, may I draw you."

Liam nodded.

A pair of shadows drifted over and stood above them. Ethan and Noah. Listening.

"My son has started doing faces," Ryan explained. "He told me this morning he likes yours."

"A lot," Liam said. Quiet. Not meeting her gaze.

Jenna took her time responding. "I am honored. Truly. But I have to ask one thing. Only I'm not asking, not really. This is an either/or. Do you understand what I mean when I say that?"

Ryan said, "She means you either agree to what she's saying or you can't draw her."

Liam lifted his gaze. Gave a fractional nod.

"I can't have you putting my face together with dead people or zombies or ghouls. It's too close to my end-care work. I never, ever want to know something like that is out there."

Liam nodded slowly. "Okay."

"Then I'd love to sit for you." Jenna rose to full height. "Soon as Noah and I have a little word."

Ten fifteen in the morning and already the day was searingly hot. A sullen breeze blew from the west, carrying the hint of sorrel and creosote. One glimpse of the jagged scar still dominating the ridgeline was enough to have Jenna yearning for early September rains.

Jenna's walk with Noah followed the same path she and Sol had taken. She hoped the dry heat and its vague hint of old ashes was not a portent of things to come.

She had so little experience with men. Almost nothing formed a hopeful pattern she might follow here. She knew what she wanted. Not even this vague disquiet pushed her to change course.

If only she knew how to begin.

In the end, though, it was Noah who finally broke the silence. "I want you to share in this. I don't know how, I can't even say if it's a good idea. Not the sharing, just taking part in everything the boat needs doing." He glanced over, clearly worried. "I feel like every time I talk with you, it comes out wrong."

"Why do I make you nervous?"

He huffed a breath. "Because you're special. Because I like you."

Jenna tasted a pleasant flavor on the air. A spice she could not even name. "Thank you, Noah."

"I feel like a teenager, stumbling over everything I say."

She loved how the space between them was clear now, an open road to whatever came next. "I've had two experiences with serious relationships. Both of them were awful."

"Don't look to me for advice. My last two didn't end up all that well. My former partner, the guy I considered my lifelong friend, maneuvered behind my back and stole my company. The other relationship ended in divorce."

She had to smile. "Third time lucky?"

"Let's hope so." His own smile was canted, the gaze somewhat fractured. But real just the same. "For both our sakes."

They walked on in silence. Then, "Jenna, you need to understand what I'm facing here. If you decide to change your mind, I totally understand."

"I won't."

"I've run my base calculations by Wallace, our boat guy. He agrees with my preliminary estimates. Even if we go for less than top-quality replacements, we're looking at an outlay of another three quarters of a million dollars. That's on top of everything I've already spent."

"I have money. Not that much. But some."

But Noah persisted. "We don't even know if this boat will float in the end."

"It will. It has to."

Noah sighed. Started to speak. Closed his mouth. Sighed again.

It was the simplest thing in the world to tell this man, this almost stranger, about Millie. The half sister Jenna knew for only a few months. A time so precious she was willing to accept Millie's unfulfilled dreams as her own. Take up a new profession, accept this as her calling. Alter her life's course in the process. Willingly. And feel richer as a result. All so she could be here. Walking down a dusty farm track, heading toward a fire-blackened ridge, sharing her life's secrets with a man she scarcely knew.

When she finished, Noah walked on for what seemed like forever. And finally responded with the single soft word, "Wow."

Jenna nodded. Wow certainly worked for her. "Maybe we should start back."

Jenna enjoyed the work more than she thought possible.

The heat was fierce. Noah insisted they stop around eleven each morning, take a long pause, rest well, eat well, drink constantly. The afternoon winds were like standing inside a giant blow-dryer. Jenna loved it just the same. She often took her breaks standing beneath the barn's shadows, watching the cottonwood leaves spin and twirl. Their silver-green dance and the meadow's dry, whispering chorus, it spoke to her. Moments like these, Jenna often thought she could sense Millie standing there, enjoying this glimpse at their shared dream.

Nine days later, Sol arrived with the papers assigning her a forty-nine percent interest in the yacht.

Jenna had already transferred most of her savings to what was now their joint boat account. Seated there at the trestle table in the waning light of another sweltering day, she felt weightless. Slightly detached from the yard and the papers awaiting her signature. She tucked her legs under the bench, gripping the wood with her calves. As if this hold was all that kept her from floating away.

Sol sat across from her, trying to remain utterly still. His eyes shifted back and forth, from Jenna to where Liam knelt farther along her bench, sketching the attorney in profile. "How long do I have to sit like this?"

"Not long. Liam is a quick draw."

"Half of my face is going to be burned."

"He likes to draw people in profile. He says the shadows talk to him."

Sol's gaze drifted back to the massive shape mostly sheltered beneath the barn's shade. "I never did understand the fascination with boats."

Jenna liked being able to study him like this. As if she observed with piercing clarity, sharing Liam's intense concentration. "Are you married?"

"Thirty-seven years next month."

"Kids?"

"Three. My baby girl graduates from USC law school next spring. I'm hoping she'll join us. But she feels the big-city lure. Four grandkids. A joy."

"I'm happy for you, Sol. If anyone deserves joy, it's you."

"What a kind thing to say, Jenna." A pause, then, "I thought we were discussing the boat."

"It's never been about a boat, Sol. It's about passions and lifelong dreams. Logic isn't the driving force here. It can't be."

He gave that the moment it deserved, then asked, "How is it working with Noah?"

"He's a leader," she replied. "It's his gift."

"You like him."

"Yes, and that's not what we're talking about. Well, it is, but not in the way . . . Noah can go all day without issuing a single order. He makes requests. He is constantly grateful. He's the kindest man I've ever met. And people will do anything for him. Even show up early and spend every possible free hour working on a boat most suspect will never be seaworthy."

Which was when Liam announced, "All done."

Jenna watched him shut his drawing pad and start to leave the table. As usual. "Shouldn't you thank Sol and show him what you've done?"

Liam stopped, one foot on the ground, like he was preparing to spring away. "Thanks."

"Sol was nice enough to hold still in this heat," Jenna insisted. "Showing him is the polite thing to do."

Liam opened his pad, found the page, slid it slowly across the table.

Jenna watched Sol's eyes go wide. "This is . . . Can I have it?"

"If he'll let it go, which doesn't happen often, Liam's sketches go for thirty dollars. Ryan's rules." She watched Liam retract his pad and walk away. "Maybe next time."

"Is he always this quiet?"

"Liam talks when he needs to."

Sol stared at the empty space on the table. "Sign the documents, Jenna."

*   *   *

At some point deep in the night, Noah had the dream that had plagued so many of his last nights in LA.

It began in the same way, a swirling collage of images, him working on a project that was late, and he couldn't get the materials, and the studio was threatening him with dismissal. Everyone on the set was stressed and angry. Just the same, he knew he had to leave. Walk away from this huge project at a critical moment. Because he was due in court.

The dream shifted. He was seated in the corridor outside the courtroom. The bench was hard as iron, it dug into his back, but Noah couldn't move. His attorney was inside, arguing with the judge, fighting against the inevitable. Noah could somehow see through the closed doors. He knew he was about to lose everything. He should be in there fighting with her. But he couldn't move.

His gaze shifted. And he realized Elaine, his ex-wife, was seated there beside him. She held the divorce papers. And a pen. She reached out. "Here. Sign."

But Noah couldn't even move his hand. The documents slipped out of his lap. The pen rattled like a lonely drum as it struck the tiled floor. He stared down at the pages now spread around his feet. Helpless.

Elaine drew his attention back with, "One question."

That phrase, *One question*, was how their deepest conversations had often begun. In his dream, Noah studied her in the light of divorce. A woman who for him was only yesterday. Noah wondered if he managed to carry his pain as well as she did. Stoic, calm, hurting, but determined to heal. And so lovely.

Noah heard himself say, "Anything."

His ex-wife asked, "Did you ever want children?"

At that point, as always, Noah woke up.

He lay there in the dark, listening to the valley's soft night sounds through his open window, remembering how the dream's aftermath had assaulted him back in LA. Waking up bathed in sweat, feeling lost and helpless and alone and . . .

Reduced to a burned-out, exhausted hulk.

Noah rose from his bed, padded barefoot into the kitchen, and poured himself a glass of water. The ancient fridge hummed and rattled. He unlatched the screen door and stepped onto the porch. The wind had cooled now, the air filled with clean, dry California flavors. He leaned against the railing and breathed deep. Remembering how things once had been, everything he had lost in the process. He was so grateful for this place and its healing winds. It felt as though he had left LA years ago, rather than just a few weeks. The open-sided barn cut a massive silhouette from the night.

The bow jutted out, a huge unfinished sculpture. Noah relished the coming day, the work and the sweat and the friends there to call on.

And Jenna.

The thought of her was enough to spark his chest with a very real fear. The lady continued to pull at the locked and hidden doors. He yearned for a closer relationship with this lady, almost as much as the prospect frightened him.

That was when Noah heard the sound.

A soft clink. A hiss. Then nothing.

"Hello?" Noah couldn't be certain, but he thought the noise came from the barn. "Who's there?"

Nothing.

For the first time since he had moved into the farmhouse, he fretted over the surrounding darkness. He reentered the kitchen, opened the drawer by the sink, and found the police-grade flashlight Amos had given him as a housewarming present. A place this old and poorly maintained, Amos had told him, losing power was a constant. The flashlight was sixteen inches long and weighed almost a pound and a half. It was encased in black rubber, molded into ridges for grip. Unbreakable plexiglass lens. Powerful as a searchlight.

Noah returned to the porch and swept the light over the barn. "Who's out there?"

He hesitated, wondering if he should call Amos. But that seemed so lame, the citified brother frightened by a sound. It could have been a fox, anything. Or just his imagination. Noah forced himself down the steps and started across the backyard.

Then far off in the distance, he heard the rattling clamor of a dirt bike climbing the ridge.

CHAPTER 18

Noah told Jenna about his midnight scare over coffee the next morning. She heard him out, then asked, "What did Amos say?"

"I haven't told him."

She straightened, almost coming out of her rocker. "Are you nuts?"

"What if it's nothing? I feel kind of silly even telling you."

She rose to her feet as he spoke. "Where is your phone?"

"Kitchen table."

She entered the house and returned. Extended her arm. Planting the phone in his face. "Call him."

"Jenna . . ."

"Did it sound to you like I was making a suggestion? Something we can stand around and discuss?" She wiggled the phone. "Call your brother, Noah." She crossed her arms, watched him hit speed dial. "I can't believe we're actually having this conversation."

Neither, apparently, could Amos. "Why am I only hearing about this now?"

Noah felt Jenna's glare on him, strong as the day's rising heat. "I started to call you this morning. But then I saw you peel out of here in a hurry. I figured . . . Tell the truth, I thought it might be, you know . . ."

"A robber?" Jenna's voice carried a real anger. "Somebody armed and dangerous?"

Amos asked, "That Jenna?"

"She made me call." Sounding to his own ears like a sullen teen.

"Give the lady a gold star. You and I, now, we're going to have words. Have you been inside the boat?"

"Right after I woke up. Nothing's missing that I can tell."

"It's not about you checking, Noah. It's about preserving a potential crime scene."

"Come on, Amos. What if it was just a neighbor's dog?"

"Do you even hear yourself?" Amos's tone matched Jenna's glare. "You have a boat that was torn apart, then sunk. The perps have vanished. Now you have a possible B&E where the culprit escapes on a trail bike."

"I heard a motor in the distance," Noah replied. "I have no way of connecting—"

"This is ridiculous," Jenna said.

Amos said, "You sound as lame as my daughter coming in after curfew. Stay clear of the barn. Zia and I will be out directly."

"I've got a hundred things to get done today—"

"Stay away from the boat, Noah. Don't go tracking more footprints. Take the lady to lunch. We'll swing by in a couple of hours. Hand her the phone, will you. I need to have a word with an adult."

Jenna watched Noah cut the connection and rise to his feet. He gave the barn a long look, then told her, "We're officially barred from going anywhere near our boat. If I stick around here, I'll go nuts. Buy you an early lunch?"

It was far from the most charming invitation she'd ever received. "Sounds good."

Noah didn't speak again until they were entering the diner. "You're right. I should have called Amos. Soon as I heard the bike climb the ridge."

She slid into a window booth opposite Noah and facing the door. She accepted a menu from the waitress. She liked how easy it felt, like they had been friends for years. Like she was ready . . .

For what, exactly?

Noah ordered a burger with slaw on the side, hold the fries. She went for the tuna melt. When the waitress was gone, she wondered if now was a good moment to talk about what they had been putting off. Her money, their new joint account, the stages still required to make the boat seaworthy, and what was coming after. She liked how natural it had all felt up to that point. Just moving from day to day, filling their time together with the next task. Enjoying his company and the sweaty work and the sunshine and the valley, all of it.

Looking back, it seemed to Jenna as if everything changed in an instant. As if the shift was already there in the booth before they arrived. And it all started by her asking the simplest of questions. "Will you tell me about your work in Hollywood?"

Noah waited while the waitress set down their drinks— raspberry ice tea for her, black coffee for Noah. He fiddled with the spoon he didn't need, then said, "I always thought I'd have more time."

She must have jerked. Some response strong enough to draw his attention. She told him, "You don't know how often I've heard those words."

Noah had the most remarkable eyes. Not gray so much as pewter, with a burnished quality, as if illuminated from within. "You mean, from your patients."

"A few say they're ready. One or two even seem glad." She smiled at a sudden memory. "One patient, a university English professor, put it this way: 'Off with this mortal coil. I want to have tea with Emily and share a dark ale with the Bard himself.' Those were the last words she spoke."

"Wow."

"Something, huh."

"I wish I could be that eloquent. You know, when it matters." He went back to fiddling with his spoon. "I've often thought that's how it felt. Losing my company was a lot like a small death."

"Not to mention your wife." When he did not respond, she said, "I'm sorry. I shouldn't have brought that up."

"Three years of counseling, four separations before we finally called it quits." He set down the spoon, lifted his mug, took a long sip. "Amos met her once. All it took for him to know the truth."

"Dare I ask?"

"Elaine wanted what I could never give."

She was quiet a long moment, but not because of his words. Not really. Jenna needed to take stock. The way she leaned forward, so close she could see a small dark patch on his left jawline where he had not shaved properly. The creases that had appeared now as he thought about his ex, the tight furrows spreading out from his eyes. The sorrow. "Which was . . ."

"Life on a pedestal. First place in her husband's mind and heart and life. Just like her dad treated her mother." Noah met her gaze. "Why couldn't I see that for myself?"

"Because you were in love."

"It wasn't enough. Loving her."

"That doesn't mean you were in the wrong. Neither of you."

He breathed tight little puffs of air, sharing the coffee scent. "Amos said pretty much the same thing."

Then she realized the waitress was standing there, plates in hand. Jenna leaned back, breaking the connection. They ate a few bites in silence. Then, "Thank you for sharing this with me, Noah."

"You asked about my work and look where it took us."

They did not speak again until their meals were finished. Then Jenna asked, easy as mentioning the weather, "Speaking of work. Does my profession bother you?"

"No." Noah pushed his plate to one side. Clearing the decks. Almost like he had been waiting for the question. Or perhaps, he'd been thinking about that very thing. "On one level it unsettles me. Some."

"There's a difference?"

"Absolutely. For me, at least. The way you said it. Does it bother me? That sounded like I'm repelled. If that's what you meant, then no, Jenna. Absolutely not."

"But you're unsettled."

"What you see, the people you clearly care for, watching them and being with them right to that very last breath." He shook his head. "Wow."

She loved it. Just could not get enough of this. Being with this handsome, wounded man, surrounded by the clatter and chatter of a busy diner, lost in the moment. Together. "What, wow."

"Am I allowed to say that would totally creep me out?"

"You can say whatever you want." She found herself moving her own plate to one side. So she could lean closer. Watching as Noah did the same. "But you're not, as you say, disturbed."

"There is a depth to you, a calm. It has to come from your work. I think about that sometimes. You know . . ."

"Tell me."

"At night. When I feel like the past starts to close in. I think about what I see in your eyes, Jenna. Like now."

She felt herself clench slightly. It felt that good. She repeated, "Tell me."

"It's like staring into a bottomless pool of utterly calm water. Like I could just fall in and go deeper and deeper. Forever."

She did her best to suppress a tight shiver. "Sometimes at night, you know, after I'm back home and recovering from another departure . . ."

When she went quiet, it was Noah's turn to say, "Tell me."

"I feel like this is what I was made for. Reaching out in ways that are uniquely mine. Soothing away the loneliness, the lack of control . . ."

This time, when she stopped and searched for the right word, it was Noah who said, "The terror."

"That's what I see sometimes. Yes. How did you know?"

"It's what I feel, reliving my life coming apart. I'm left facing the empty black hour."

"The empty black hour," she repeated. Wow. "I feel like what I do is most special then. Being a friend to the end."

"That's how you described it when we were all eating together. I've thought a lot about that. What it must mean to, you know, your patients."

"I don't want them ever to feel alone."

"A friend to the end." Noah clenched down tight then. Almost like he was struggling not to weep. But he did not pull away. When he finally spoke, his voice sounded choked. "There've been times when I could have used that."

She started to point out how many people were around him now. Sharing their few free hours with him and his boat. But she sensed they had gone as far as they needed to, or should. At least for now. Jenna smiled, leaned back, and merely said, "Perhaps we should go."

CHAPTER 19

They were midway back to the valley when Noah started in, his manner as easy as he'd been in the diner. "My step-mother was okay. We never really connected, you know, like what Ethan and Liam have. It's great to see, but sometimes I wonder what life might have been like."

"It's alien to you," Jenna said, scooting over so she could lean on the door and watch him. "What about your father?"

"Dad was a microbiologist. He pretty much worked all the time." Noah offered her a canted grin. "Wonder who that reminds you of, right?"

She let the words drift out the open window, watched his face lose the old creases. Let the silence work its calming magic. It was either that or reach out and hold him. Which she wanted to. Very much. "So your homelife . . ."

"My stepmom showed up with two daughters from a previous marriage. I have nothing in common with my step-sisters. They're both doctors. Studied all the time. Only reason we exchanged Christmas cards was because my ex had them on her list. One of them showed up for our wedding. The other . . ." He dismissed them with a wave of his hand. "I know absolutely nothing about my stepmom's first husband, except he's alive and not part of the picture." He turned onto the ranch road and continued. "I had zero interest in college. But my dad offered me a bribe. Go for a year, get good grades, if it didn't stick he'd help me do whatever . . ."

A sheriff's ride and Zia's unmarked police vehicle were parked in front of the farmhouse. As Noah pulled in and cut the motor, the two friends appeared from the barn's shadows. Even at this distance Jenna could see they were worried.

Noah said, "Something's wrong."

Noah watched the two officers walk toward them, talking softly, faces set in lines that spelled trouble. The softly intimate bond he'd known with Jenna vanished swift as dust in a rising wind. He could almost watch it sweep down the valley and out of sight.

Truth be told, he had no idea how he felt about it. On the one hand, their conversation was as fine a shared moment as he'd known in a very long time. On the other, he felt himself being drawn so far out of his comfort zone he couldn't even name where or when he'd crossed the line. This woman, his partner in the boat, and now . . . What?

Which led to the other questions. The ones he'd successfully avoided. Until now.

What exactly did he want? Was he ready for another relationship? Did he want it with Jenna?

He had no idea.

Noah asked, "Did you find anything?"

"Your fresh tracks. A lot of others that might mean something. Or not."

"I mean, like a fox or some other animal."

Amos shook his head. "Hard to tell, with all the dogs we've had around here."

"So . . . It could be nothing."

"That's not the point. Describe for me what happened."

"I woke up, got a glass of water, took it out on the porch. Like I said. Just stood there watching the night, when I heard something. Or not."

"Forget the not," Amos ordered. "Go on."

"There was a clink. Like metal on metal. I'm pretty sure it came from the barn. So I called out. Then I went inside and got your flashlight. I came back out, called again. Then I heard the bike." He pointed farther down the ridge, back where the trees marked the valley's end. "I'm pretty sure it came from around there."

Zia asked, "Are you armed?"

"What? No."

Zia said, "Man needs a gun."

Amos shook his head. "Not if he can't shoot, he doesn't. Not unless he wants to put more holes in that boat of his." To Noah, "Next time you even *think* you've heard something, what are you going to do?"

"Call you."

"That's step one. Step two?"

"Stay away from the boat."

"Long as we understand each other." He motioned for Jenna to join them. "Officer Morales has something he'd like to say."

Zia frowned at nothing in particular. "I thought maybe I should do a little checking."

"What he means to say is, he stirred the hornet's nest," Amos said. "Zia is good at that."

"You think maybe I could get on with this? I'm on the clock here."

"Just trying to clarify the situation."

"Anyway, the family ordered an autopsy of your guy."

Amos said, "We're talking about the late great Dino Vicenza."

"Right. Apparently the family specifically instructed the docs to check for any sign of, you know, foul play. Overdose, wrong meds, the works."

Noah watched her tense up. Heard her say, "There's nothing to find."

"Steady, now," Amos said. "That's not why we're here."

"These days, a full work-up requires fingerprinting and DNA," Zia said. "Turns out, your patient isn't who he claimed to be."

"I'm sorry, what?"

"Until the early sixties," Zia said, "One Dino Vicenza was known as Benny Watts."

Jenna took a step back. "I don't understand."

Amos said, "Apparently your former patient was an Italian by way of the Israeli clan."

Zia went on. "Benny Watts was an accountant out of Chicago. One day he ups and vanishes."

This time, it was Noah who said, "What does this have to do with us?"

Frowning was apparently Zia's way of handling discomfort. "We're not exactly clear on that point."

"Apparently the FBI received an automatic red-flag alert on your man's fingerprints," Amos said. "So they're still coming to terms with how this guy has just popped onto their radar after having disappeared years back. Then three minutes later . . ."

"It was longer than that," Zia said.

"All right. Ten. While they're trying to figure out exactly what's going on, they get a hit on their system, a certain San Lu cop asking questions about a man they assumed had been dead for decades." Amos crossed his arms. Gave Zia a hard stare. "Man just couldn't let the thing go."

Zia kicked at a rock lodged deep in the earth by his feet. "I asked a buddy on the Santa Barbara force to keep me apprised. How was I to know—"

"A rich dude like that, fake identity his family apparently had no idea was even there, you go and ask questions." Amos shook his head. "You beat all."

"Whatever. Thing is, a federal agent is on his way here. He wants to have a word."

Jenna protested, "I don't know anything."

"That's never stopped the feds," Zia replied.

"Agent Wright Manley Banks," Amos said. "Just about the whitest name I've ever come across."

Zia pointed to a dust cloud approaching from the valley's entry. "Here comes trouble."

CHAPTER 20

Agent Wright Manley Banks was combat lean, a body so lacking in fat his shirt and suit trousers lumped around the muscles of his shoulders, the corded neck, the bony hips. His cheeks were shadowed by a beard that needed a mid-afternoon shave. He handed Jenna a business card while holding out his leather ID case for her inspection. Banks frowned when Amos and Zia both insisted on checking his creds. "I'd like to ask you a few questions regarding the late Benjamin Watts."

"If you're talking about who I think you are, I'd prefer to call him Dino. It's the only name I ever knew him by. I guess his family must have told you the same thing. This earlier name comes as a total shock."

Banks turned to where Zia and Amos and Noah hovered. "I'd like to have a private word with Ms. Greaves."

"See, now, that's fine," Amos replied. "Long as privacy is what Ms. Greaves herself wants."

"Stay," Jenna told them. "Please."

"What the lady says, that goes," Zia said.

Banks shook his head. "That is unacceptable."

"Which is a decision you don't have the power to make," Amos replied.

The agent turned to Jenna. "Maybe we should continue this interview in our Santa Barbara offices."

"Here is fine," Jenna replied. "With them."

"Ms. Greaves, it would be in your long-term interests to cooperate," Banks told her. "We can make this a lot more uncomfortable for everyone concerned, believe me."

Zia bristled. He asked Amos, "Did that sound like a threat to you? Because I definitely picked up on something."

"Carried a bit of that flavor, sure enough."

Zia turned back to the agent. "This coming from a fed whose agency let a guy slip for sixty-plus years."

Amos added, "Which brings us to the real point. Why is this guy, currently deceased, of any interest to the FBI?"

Banks had eyes the color of dirty snow, dark gray with black flecks, and blank as a steel door. "See, this is why we at the FBI love working with local law enforcement."

"Oh, the feeling is mutual, believe me," Zia replied.

"Ask your questions to the lady," Amos said. "So we can usher you right on out of here."

Jenna directed them to the trestle table, partially shaded by the barn. Banks watched the three other men take their places, his expression pinched, like he was being forced to munch on a bad lemon. Jenna did not look directly at Noah. She didn't know if her feelings would be evident. But she didn't want to show the agent what it meant to have Noah settle down beside her. Close enough she could feel his comforting strength. And heat. She liked that enough to ask, "What can I do for you?"

Banks was seated across from her. He set his phone on the table between them. "You mind if I record this conversation?"

"Not at all."

Amos was stationed farther down, Zia in a chair at the far end. Amos set his phone on the table. "What an excellent idea."

Banks's features tightened further. But he did not look over. "You were with Mr. . . . Vicenza for how long?"

"Almost nineteen months."

"After his demise, you remained in the house another . . ."

"Fifteen days. Until probate ended."

"And this happened because . . ."

"Dino, Mr. Vicenza, asked me to remain. Serve as co-executor of his estate. I didn't want to. But Dino made it his dying request. I didn't feel I could refuse."

"Why didn't you want to perform this final duty, Ms. Greaves?"

"I assume you've already spoken to Dino's family."

He nodded. "I understand you were well paid for what was apparently a very easy duty."

"Two thousand dollars a day," she confirmed. "Just the same, I wish I had refused."

"Because . . ."

"You've met them. Dino's survivors."

"Could you clarify what you mean by that?"

"No, I don't have anything further to say about any of them."

"Ms. Greaves, I require—"

Amos interrupted, "The lady has given you all she wants to. I suggest you move on."

Jenna could see Banks was ready to argue. She diffused the situation with, "One of my rules is to never get between the patient and their family."

"Interesting. You have a lot of rules like that?"

"My job isn't as carefully defined as most nursing duties. I've had to form a structure of my own."

"So this rule of yours. It didn't work here, did it. From what I understand, you served as a permanent barrier between the late Vicenza-Watts and his surviving family."

Jenna could see both Amos and Zia were increasingly irritated by the agent's questions. And Noah. His body was so tight she could easily see him leaping across the table, taking the agent by the throat. She said to the three men, "It's okay."

"Seems to me, we should hold off until we can get Sol up here," Amos growled. "Teach this agent here the proper way to address a voluntary witness."

Noah rose from the table, glaring at the agent, who continued to ignore them all. Pretending he was immune to the general hostility. Noah said, "I'll give Sol a call."

"No." Jenna reached for his hand. Liking how she was sheltered by these three men. All of whom had until recently been strangers. Now, though . . .

Friends.

She pulled Noah back down. Said to them all, "He's just doing his job."

Once Noah was settled, closer now than before, she turned back. Banks watched her with a different slant to his features. The hostility was still there. But added to this was a measure of caution. Uncertainty. Something. Jenna told him, "The second day I was in Dino's employ, he gave me strict instructions that none of his family were to be allowed inside his home."

"Did he say why?"

"He didn't need to. Sol had warned me that relations between Dino and his family were . . . not good."

"That would be Sol Feinnes, attorney in San Luis Obispo. You know him how?"

"Sol has served as my attorney since my mother passed, that was almost ten years ago. He's also a friend."

Banks tapped the table with one finger. Again. "Did Mr. . . . Vicenza ever discuss his past?"

"Dino was one of the most private people I ever met. A complete anomaly. The answer is no."

"Anomaly how?"

"Most people who know they are approaching the end want nothing more than to relive elements from their past. Things they regret. Happy memories. Children and milestones. The topics shift from person to person. I think . . ."

"Yes? I'm curious. What do you think?"

Jenna found it increasingly easy to ignore the man's hostile suspicion. "They use memories to keep hold of life as it slips away. Their focus can't be forward. Nobody knows what lies beyond that final door. And that frightens my patients, some more than others. The past becomes far clearer than the now. My job is to listen."

"And Watts . . . Dino?"

"He only spoke about his past one time." She briefly described Dino's account of driving contraband booze across the frozen Lake Michigan.

When she went silent, Banks demanded, "Surely there must have been something more."

"Not once. Not ever."

Banks looked ready to press, then started to glance down the table. Caught himself. "Your most recent contact with the family was . . ."

"Yesterday. My last ever. Definitely."

"That was for . . ."

"The reading of the will."

"There was the matter of a hidden safe."

"Filled with gold bullion. As you've probably been informed."

"Who took possession of that gold?"

"I have no idea."

"And you were present because . . ."

"All the home's locks are controlled through the same master panel that handles the alarms. When Dino decided he could trust me, he had my thumbprint added to the control system. I had no idea that included a safe in the wine cellar."

"For real?" Zia brightened. "The old man stashed gold with his booze?"

Banks looked ready to bark, but Jenna lifted one hand in time to halt his outburst. Settle. She went on. "They accused me of stealing some of the funds. Sol will tell you the safe was completely full. There was nothing I could have taken."

"So you say."

"Yes, Agent Banks. That is what I say."

"What happened then?"

"I have no idea. I opened the safe. I stood. I left the premises. And I am never, ever going back."

Agent Wright Manley Banks continued to press her with questions, going over the same points from different directions, for almost an hour. His tone remained suspicious, aggressive. Jenna didn't care. She found herself entering the same observant calm she knew when tending a patient. Nothing that happened on the outside disturbed her inner world. It couldn't, not if Jenna was going to do the best by her patient. This agent might think he was searching for her button, something he could press and gain a reaction that might lead to Jenna divulging a secret. But she had no secret to reveal, and his hostile questioning left her utterly untouched.

As for Noah, Amos, and Zia, it was like watching three pots slowly rise to a boil.

Agent Banks pressed for her impressions of each family member. Asked about known associates. Everyone who visited or called during Dino's final months.

Then he insisted on seeing the boat.

"Absolutely not," Noah said.

This time, however, Amos sided with Jenna. "Give the man a tour. Else he'll be back with a warrant and waste another afternoon. This way he won't bother us again."

Banks rose to his feet. "Don't bet on it."

They climbed into the boat, watched him nose around. Then it was over.

Agent Banks departed with a barely polite thanks for her time. "If you think of anything further, please give us a call."

"About what? You still haven't told me what you were looking for."

"There you go," Amos said.

Banks opened his car door, shot the three men a hard look, said, "We'll be in touch."

When the agent's nondescript four-door was just a dust cloud headed for the valley's gates, Noah asked her, "You okay?"

"I'm fine."

Amos said, "You need to give Sol a heads-up."

"In a minute." Jenna started toward Zia, who had walked back across the rear yard, frowning into the harsh afternoon light. Clearly waiting for her or Amos or Noah to give him a hard time.

Soon as she got within range, Zia started in with, "My wife keeps telling me I'm a master at doing the wrong thing for all the right reasons. She . . ."

Jenna embraced him, silencing the man. "You are a very good man."

Amos walked over. "If the lady is giving out hugs, I volunteer to be next."

Jenna stepped back far enough to see all three of them. Standing there, ignoring the heat, watching her. Making sure she was okay. The first thing on their minds. "That agent would have come looking for me. Sooner rather than later. Every single one of Dino's kin would be falling over themselves, blaming me for everything under the sun."

Amos nodded. "Lady's got a point."

She told Zia, "If you hadn't made your search, he might have caught me when I was alone and vulnerable and scared. Your alert helped me more than I will ever say."

Zia was watching her now. "So . . . we're good?"

"We're better than that." She hugged him again. "You know I'm half owner of this boat."

"I think I mighta heard that somewhere."

"Anytime, anywhere. I'm serious. You, your family, the entire San Lu police force. It's yours for the asking."

Noah asked, "Do I have a say in the matter?"

Jenna kept her gaze on Zia. "No."

CHAPTER 21

That evening, Noah was washing up after a solitary meal. The sun was below the western horizon, the sky filled with streaks of copper and gold. He was weary in a manner that took him back to nights in LA. Usually he'd arrived home well after dark. He remembered what it was like, pulling into the drive of a home where he had never really felt comfortable. He'd be talking on the speakerphone, making plans for the next day. Working over a last-minute problem. Something. The house would be lit from within and without, a pristine sculpture that left him feeling like he didn't belong. The good feeling of work done well was gradually replaced by tension. Preparing for whatever might be awaiting him inside that huge front door.

He felt that way now.

The boat gleamed soft and ruddy in the fading light. Noah pushed through the screen door and crossed the rear lawn. He did a slow circuit around the barn, studying his craft from every angle. Only now it did not feel like his. It felt . . .

The agent's hard-edged attitude was compounded by the

previous night's unanswered questions. He turned and stared out over the far ridge, wondering what he had heard, who had been out there dirt-biking without lights. At three in the morning.

There was something else at work here. Something big.

Noah took his time, circling the barn, inspecting the boat's pristine hull. The walk took him straight back, clearly as if he were standing on the periphery of a half-finished set. Working through what needed to happen for a successful shoot, and when. Only now he worked over the missing element. Something that left him uneasy within his own skin.

He climbed the wooden stairs and stood on the upper platform, surrounded by Ethan's tools. The banker-woodworking artist was due back the next morning. The air was filled with the scent of fresh-cut wood. The lower deck and interior flooring were coming along well. No question. The boat was taking shape.

Others might see a total disaster zone, a construction site surrounded by refuse and tools and unfinished jobs. But Noah's professional career had depended upon his ability to look beyond all that. Determine everything that was needed to complete the job, on budget and on time.

See the finished project. And beyond.

Which was what Noah was doing now. Looking beyond the build. To . . . What?

Work had reached a point where he could see the finished craft. Money was the big issue now. Not just how much they needed to complete the work. Upkeep and maintenance on such a craft was hugely expensive.

But that wasn't what troubled him.

He had a momentary image of them launching the boat. Climbing on board. And setting off.

Together.

Despite the day's lingering heat, Noah shivered.

This should have been a moment of unbridled joy. Instead, all Noah could see ahead were doubts and questions. And fears. A huge number of fears. Starting with, what on earth was he doing? Building a boat? To do what, exactly? Run away? Cross the Pacific in search of a new life?

Well, yes.

This project was surrounded by the hope that here, in this work, he would rebuild not just a craft but the wreckage of his own life.

Only now that the next step was in sight, he was terrified.

And it wasn't the boat.

It was Jenna.

Then his brother called from the dark, startling Noah from his reverie. "In here."

Amos held a lead that clinked as he crossed the yard. On the lead's other end was a dog.

A very big dog.

"This is Bear."

"He sure looks like one."

"Bear is half Mastiff, half Great Dane, and all teddy bear." Amos scratched the massive head. "Bear is seventeen, same age as my older daughter. The girls have grown up with the beast. They treat him like he's still their puppy. One or the other will show up around dusk and take him for walks. Now there's nothing much left but his bark and his appetite. But if your home invaders return, they won't know that."

"If there is one."

"Get serious." Amos motioned him forward. "Bear, give Noah your paw."

It was like holding a padded dinner plate. With claws.

"If you hear a foghorn blast in the night, it's Bear. Now come give me a hand."

Amos tied Bear's lead to the rear porch and walked back to the sheriff's ride. Noah asked, "Would it do any good to object?"

"There's nothing you can object to. You might have had a break-in you stopped by the skin of your teeth. You're out here at the end of the valley road, completely isolated. You need a guard dog." Amos opened his trunk. "Grab one of those sacks."

Noah hefted a fifty-pound sack of feed and carried it back to the porch. Waited while Amos returned for a pair of hard rubber bowls the size of tureens. "Feed him twice a day. Give him a good rub. Here." Amos handed him a lead that had to be eighty feet long. Coiled like a rancher's rope. "Fasten that to the strongest of the barn pillars."

"Amos . . ."

He had already started back toward the car. Turned. The silhouette showed a man ready for a scrap. "What."

Noah could see he had already lost the battle. "Thank you."

"Take him for a walk when you feel like it. You'll have a friend for life." Amos climbed behind the wheel. "I'm late for dinner."

Noah watched the car's lights crawl back down the central road. Halt in front of a house by the gates. Heard voices. A girl's high-pitched laughter.

He turned back to the dog and the strengthening night.

And the questions about Jenna.

He had no idea what to do.

CHAPTER 22

Noah prepared for bed that night thinking about Jenna. As usual. She had come to dominate his solitary hours, the thoughts so intense she might have been in the room. Wherever he went, whatever he did, Jenna followed. Silent in the way that was unique to her. Special. The calm eyes, the woman's quiet spirit.

He knew the building tension was all his. She did not push. She did not ask him questions that they both needed to work through. The boat, the day, the future, all of it pressed on him.

He was so scared.

The building emotions, the bonds growing between them, all brought him face-to-face with his unhealed wounds.

Next month marked four full years since his and Elaine's first separation. The anger and hurt and frustration were not just memories of a very bad time. They were with him still. Adding to the latent fear that he might not be ready. That he would wind up making the same mistakes all over again.

He did not try to tell himself he was worried for Jenna's sake. How he might hurt a good woman through no fault of hers.

Tempting. But no.

This was a selfish fear, and three years of therapy had left him able to confront it honestly. He was afraid of hurting himself all over again. Afraid he didn't have the strength to go through yet another disastrous end to a relationship that should never have been allowed to start. Or grow to the point where it was now. Relying on her for so much. She was part of it all now. His dream, the boat, and his tomorrow. Each step had seemed so natural. And yet as he faced the *next* step, the *next* move, the transition into real love . . .

He had no idea what to do. Or rather, he knew what he *should* do. But how? Wrench it all apart? Be partners in the boat and end the romance?

Yes. Yes.

He felt the urge growing. . . .

And yet.

Just thinking about the prospect of actually doing it left his heart aching.

Noah carried his dilemma to bed. He lay down and listened to the night sounds through his screened window. Drifting off, he wondered if perhaps there was actually no right next move. Whatever he did, it would hurt, and he would be rendered damaged and bruised all over again.

The transition from awake to sleep was so smooth Noah was not even aware it had happened. He simply carried on with his worries, only now they took the form of dreams.

He stood in the home that used to be his. Or theirs. He and his ex were arguing. As usual. The reason for this quarrel was so trivial, so unimportant, he was mostly angry about giving it time and energy. As if the outcome did not matter at all. Whether or not he won, or even if she understood why he was angry. None of that mattered. They argued. It was what they did.

In his dream, Elaine kept moving from room to room. He followed behind, using her distance as a reason to shout. Frustrated that he could not get her to just let it go, give him a chance to have a quiet night. He was so tired. Strung out from a hard and exhausting day. Abruptly he realized this was the real reason for her anger. She hated how he came home with so little to give. Wanting nothing more than a chance to kick back, relax, take an easy breath, reflect on everything that had to happen the next day.

Instead, she shouted. About what didn't matter.

He kept following Elaine from room to room. Always one step behind. She stayed just far enough ahead that he followed the sound of her voice, never actually seeing her.

Suddenly, it all changed.

He was in the farmhouse. Tracking her from one old wood-lined room to the next, maneuvering around his unpacked boxes and crates. Still shouting. He accelerated, wanting to catch her, ask her what she was doing here in this new phase of his life. . . .

He entered the kitchen. She stood by the rear window, silhouetted by the afternoon light. She turned . . .

It was Jenna.

CHAPTER 23

Jenna's days became structured around achieving Noah's goals.

On the surface, the days passed in an orderly procession. Down deep, however, Jenna knew something was seriously wrong.

Ethan took his vacation to complete work on the main deck. He was crucial to their progress now, the master artisan, the artist whose tools were wood and epoxy and polish and sweat. Jenna and Liam both served as his assistants. Ryan came and went according to her hours on duty, usually timing so as to bring the day's one main meal. Noah worked high overhead, repairing the flying bridge.

His position today was pretty much how he had remained all week. Or so it seemed to her. Always there, perpetually at a distance.

Jenna wondered if Noah was upset over how she had pressed him to contact Amos. Was he the kind of guy who couldn't take being ordered around by a woman? Her mind said no. But she could not find another decent reason to account for how he remained so distant.

Twice during that period, Bear erupted in the night.

Jenna learned about it only because Amos and Zia told her. When she asked Noah, he made light of the moments when Bear started barking, loud enough to wake Amos a quarter mile away. The second time, Zia arrived with a forensics specialist from the San Lu force. The woman made a painstaking inspection of the surroundings, took everyone's fingerprints and dusted the boat, then made plaster casts of tire tracks down by the cottonwoods at the valley's far end. Noah spent the time glancing repeatedly at his watch. But Amos's hard glare kept his brother from protesting the lost hours.

Liam became Jenna's constant companion. The youth almost never spoke. When she glanced over, even to smile or point out the next task, he almost always looked away. She assumed it was a case of puppy love, but that did not make it any less important, at least in Liam's eyes. Jenna found she did not mind his quiet attentiveness, not in the least. Especially when Ethan and Ryan both accepted her as a trusted friend, because of how she treated the young man.

Ethan's work on the main deck was a growing astonishment. Jenna viewed him with the same respect she might show a master jeweler. Every piece was meticulously measured and cut and fit into place. The result was a seamless flow. Ethan never hurried. In fact, his motions seemed painstakingly slow. But by the close of each day, another sizable portion was completed. Gradually the parlor and kitchen and master bedroom and bath all grew new floors and walls.

That morning Jenna was on her break, seated at the trestle table partly shaded by the barn's rear overhang. Liam was seated across from her, drawing her again. He had been doing this every few days, changing her position, moving her in and out of shade, using as few words as possible to get her exactly where he wanted. She actually enjoyed the sessions. She suspected more was happening than just one undersized preteen using her as a model. This was Liam's way of being close to her. She liked him. Keeping still for a while was fine.

Noah walked over, inspected them a long moment, then said, "Wallace Myers called. The kitchen appliances have arrived. And fixtures for the master bath."

"Finally."

Liam hissed softly. His way of telling her not to move.

Noah said, "I've got the electrician coming in this afternoon. We need to calibrate the flying deck instrumentation. Will you go?"

"Of course." She ignored Liam's hiss. "Soon as we're done here."

Noah stood there a moment longer.

"Was there something else?"

The air seemed to go out of him. Like he was defeated. Unable to say what had burdened him.

"Noah, what's the matter?" More silence. "Why won't you talk to me?"

He turned and started away. "Take the truck."

Jenna sat there, enveloped by the day's dry heat, worrying over what Noah had not been saying for the past ten days. Distant and stressed and, well, grim was the word that came to mind.

Then Liam broke into her thoughts by saying, "I get so afraid sometimes."

She turned her head slightly. Far enough to see how he addressed the paper and the pencil in his hand. Jenna had the impression he was in a similar situation to Noah. Letting out a fraction of what he'd been keeping bottled up inside. Since forever.

She liked having a reason to focus on something other than what Noah was refusing to let out, and said, "What about?"

"Mom." The pencil stayed busy. Pushing against the page, harder now. "Especially at night."

"Tell me why, Liam."

She could hear the pencil scratching, see the darker edge being pressed into the page. "That she'll go out one night and not come back."

Which at least partly explained his recent fascination with ghouls. She chose her words carefully. "Are you asking me what you should do?"

He bent closer to the page. Nodded.

"There's only one answer I can think of. Make friends." She watched his drawing hand slow, the motions careful, his nose almost touching the page now. "People you trust. People who might help you through these worrying times."

"Ethan says I have to talk."

She pointed out, "We're talking now. So I know you can when you want."

"It's hard."

"Especially with people you don't know, right?"

The hand stilled. "Especially with girls."

Jenna leaned closer. "Is there a girl you like?"

He breathed a name. Soft as the wind rustling the dry field. "Kimberly."

"You're worried about saying the wrong thing?"

A fractional nod.

"Does she like you?"

"She says she does."

"Then Kimberly has looked beyond your quiet nature and seen how remarkable you are." Jenna leaned closer still.

"Being uncomfortable with the opposite sex doesn't go away. Not worrying over saying the wrong thing. Not hoping they like you as much as you like them. It's there. It *stays* there."

He glanced at her. Away. "I want to say things."

"And Kimberly wants to hear what you have to say." She set a hand on the one not holding his pencil. "Hopefully she will see you as I do. Gifted. Intense. Maybe she'll recognize the elements of your remarkable character that balance out the quiet side of who you are."

Jenna heard a quiet footstep on approach. She leaned closer still, until their foreheads almost met. Wanting to hold on to this moment a bit longer. "You need to be appreciated for who you are. Not who others try to be. You are one of the most real people I have ever met. There are no masks to your nature. Someone will love you for that." She felt her throat close, sensed the emotions welling up. But this wasn't about her. She forced out the words, "Ethan and Ryan, they already know you and care deeply for you. And me. And Noah." She hated how saying that name made her eyes burn. Just hated it.

Liam slipped off the bench. Stood there a long moment, then walked away. Jenna found it difficult to unwind. She only noticed now how tense she'd become, like a watch spring that had been wound a notch too far. She wiped her face and rose slowly to discover Ethan standing there. Smiling in a mildly fractured sort of way. "I'd hug you, except for how I'm sweating enough for three."

She forced out a laugh. Started away. Embarrassed by how she could not completely hide her own fractured state. "I better be taking off."

Jenna left for Morro Bay feeling a little sad, a trifle hollow, and more than a little worried.

Jenna rarely spent time looking inward. Introspective hours like this were not usually part of her nature. But this journey south was different. She felt drawn to apply her analytical skills to what she had spent days avoiding.

Noah.

On the surface, Noah had been acting distant. Either nothing was the matter or he couldn't say what troubled him.

Couldn't or wouldn't?

Not to mention how she really did not have any business knowing more than what he wanted to tell her.

On the surface.

There had been nothing stated. The few intimate moments they'd shared had resulted in all sorts of hopes and half-formed dreams. All of which remained unspoken. And now . . .

On the surface, he treated her the same. But before she had been warmed by his closeness. Now, working with him, being around him, it made her feel like she had entered into a gray zone. Jenna hated her sense of confused helplessness.

As she entered Morro Bay township, she found herself filled with a genuine anger. Another emotion she rarely permitted herself. But this time, this moment, she had every right to be upset.

Jenna pulled into the salvage yard, cut the motor, and sat staring at the boats resting on trestles, the pair of new vessels still in their white plastic covers, the mounds of equipment. She heard the rattle of machinery through her open windows. She felt the frustration, the worry, and the sorrow that lay on a much deeper level. The real reason the day had turned colorless. Facing it for the very first time.

She loved Noah Hearst.

But she did not know him.

And she needed to. Desperately.

But to ask, to press, meant confessing her feelings out

loud. Even if she didn't say the words. Even if Noah pretended not to understand why she was asking.

Because she would know. Speaking like that, demanding answers, meant taking everything to a totally new level. Inside. Where it mattered most.

As she rose from Noah's pickup, Jenna wondered if all this confusion came down to who she was. Her total lack of experience in making a relationship work. Maybe if she had loved other men. Dived into the emotional deep end more often. Maybe then she would know what to do.

Chapter 24

Morro Bay was both a town and a convoluted stretch of coves and inlets and beaches. Shell Beach, where Jenna's anchorage was located, was five miles outside of town, a sheltered haven nestled up against a state park and wildlife preserve. Except at the height of summer, Shell Beach was a great place to be alone. Sheltered water, birds, rich golden sand, what wasn't to love.

The three main salvage yards were located south of town, where a cove cut a broad swath so far inland most locals referred to it as a creek. Which it wasn't. In the rainy season the surrounding hills drained down, but otherwise it was a deep-water cut that served the local fishing fleet and boatyards.

Myers Boats was by far the largest yard serving Morro Bay. Jenna did not particularly like Wallace Myers. Call it a gut reaction to something the man gave off when she was around. Wallace was friendly enough. He treated Jenna with an offhand courtesy. His work on the motors was first rate, according to Noah. Wallace was on time, his prices

were fair. But still. She had always felt there was a strangeness to the man and his yard. Something she could not put
her finger on.

"Well, if it isn't the lady herself." Wallace was stocky
and built low to the ground. He wore his customary outfit of cutoffs and ancient T-shirt and boat shoes. "Where's
our pal?"

"Noah couldn't get away." Jenna pretended to ignore his
outstretched hand by ducking back inside the cab for the
order sheet. She presented it with a smile. "I hope that's
okay?"

"Sure. Sure. I got everything ready to go." He took the
page and pointed toward the sliding metal doors. "Park up
over by the loading bay, why don't you."

By the time Jenna positioned the pickup, Wallace had
pulled a hand dolly from the warehouse. She could feel his
eyes on her as she lowered the rear access. She had never
liked the way Wallace tracked her. Measuring her from stem
to stern every time she came within range. But glancing
away whenever she looked his way. Just like now.

Jenna stepped back, putting the truck's rear wheel between her and the man. Making it clear she was not going to
climb up and help him load the gear. Wallace smirked, but
there was a glint of something hard in his red-rimmed eyes, a
tight rage that made a mockery of his smile.

Just the same, his tone was offhand, the words carrying a
false cheeriness. "I ought to be mad with you two. Furious.
How you and your guy proved me totally wrong."

"What are you talking about?"

"I figured Noah for the world's number one idiot, taking
on that boat." He laughed a single bark, like he wanted to
punctuate a lie with false humor. "I figured your guy, he'd
play around for a while, run out of money, then I'd buy it
for a song. Noah's made me out like ten kinds of fool."

Jenna knew he was lying. Or misdirecting. Something.

His words seemed to hold a thread that dangled just out of reach, like he was trying to tease a cat. Jenna knew she should probably let him finish loading the gear, close the rear gate, climb in, and drive off. But she was curious. She sensed a secret there in the salvage guy's eyes, how they shifted about while he talked, never touching anywhere for long, avoiding her gaze entirely.

And something else. Jenna liked having a reason not to fret over Noah and the distance between them and what it all might mean.

So she took a step farther away from where Wallace kept loading items into the pickup. And pulled on the thread. "Noah thinks the world of you and your work. Not to mention all the gear he keeps buying through your store."

Wallace kept his tone light. His hands stayed busy shifting gear. "Yeah, so here's the thing. I've been talking about your Noah and his boat. Hope that's okay."

Jenna started to correct him. Say it was their boat now. Fifty-one, forty-nine. An almost even split. But she held back. Instead, she pulled the string a little further. "Of course it's all right. Noah's doing wonderful work, isn't he? And you're helping so much."

Wallace had wiry red hair going gray, both on his head and sprouting from the neck of his T-shirt. His hands were big and dark-stained and looked permanently bruised. "So I've been telling people how your Noah's taken that wreck and made it seaworthy." Another load shifted, then, "How's the interior work coming?"

"You should see it. Ethan, our friend, he's a master craftsman with wood."

"Yeah, that's what I heard." He straightened, pretended to ease his back, squinted into the sun. "Maybe I'll come have a look tonight after I've closed up."

"Noah would love to show you around." Giving the thread another tug. "Who have you been talking to?"

"You know, clients, folks in town. People who understand what it means to do repairs like that." Back to shifting
the remaining gear. A fridge, stovetop, bathroom fixtures,
piping. "There's this guy, a lawyer retired from LA. Bought
a spread south of Lompoc, on the way to Santa Barbara.
He's rented my big craft a coupla times. Now he wants to
buy." The words tumbled out now, pushing against one another like they'd been rehearsed until they couldn't wait to
emerge. "I told him about what your Noah's been doing.
The guy is beyond eager."

Now it was her turn to play it light. Stepping away, cast-
ing a casual glance at the yard. "Eager to do what?"

"See, what your Noah's done, I told this guy it'd almost
be like buying himself a new boat for less than a fifth the
cost."

Jenna clamped down on her immediate response. That the
boat wasn't for sale. Not at any price. Their boat, their
dream. But the unspoken claim brought up all the mysteries,
the worries.

Her silence only made Wallace talk faster still. "New your
boat runs eight, almost nine mil. Sure, yours is the older version. But with less than a thousand hours on the engines, totally rebuilt, finished up nice, I think this guy might go as
high as two mil."

Jenna found it easier to stay silent. Her antennae were out.
Searching. The entire conversation was a lie. How, or why,
she couldn't say. But this wasn't about a pal interested in
buying their boat. On the face of things, Wallace's nervous
dance, the way his gaze skittered everywhere, it could all
come down to greed. But she was certain something more
was at work.

Again, her silence only made him move faster still. Bun-
dles of piping, cables for the rebuilt kitchen, finished. "You
could make some serious money here. How much do you
think Noah has in the boat?"

"Not close to that much."

"See what I mean? Noah could make a solid return on his investment. Get out clean, go for a new craft, something smaller with a totally different set of running costs. I'll chip in to make sure the interior work is first rate. Which is why I'll come up tonight. Say, seven o'clock?"

"I'll let Noah know." Jenna waited while he closed the pickup's rear gate, climbed in, started the motor, and waved through her open window.

It was only as she pulled through the yard's rusty wire fencing that it hit her. The strangeness she had not been able to identify.

There were no women. Not on his staff, or in the yard. All the visits she and Noah had made, the only women Jenna had ever seen were on the boats moored down his series of long piers. And none of those ladies had ever looked their way. Not once.

She glanced back to find Wallace still standing there on the loading dock. Fists planted on his hips. Watching. She waved again as she drove away.

CHAPTER 25

Jenna returned from Morro Bay in the late afternoon. As she drove down the long valley road, she passed Amos standing in his front yard tossing a Frisbee with his two daughters. Bear lumbered about, not coming close to catching the ball, but all of them loving how he was part of their shared moment. Heat rose in tight waves off the broken tarmac. Two other vehicles followed her, pulling into drives, raising dust. The air was very still.

When she stopped in front of the farmhouse, the place was quiet. She walked around back. "Noah?"

"In here."

She found him standing on the platform, surveying the main cabin. His shirt was streaked with sweat and dust. The still air smelled of fresh-cut wood and the epoxy Ethan used. She stood at the base of the steps, uncertain how to tell Noah what had transpired. And so much else.

Finally, Noah offered her another of those meaningless smiles. "How did it go?"

"I got everything on your manifest, if that's what you mean." When Noah's only response was to nod and turn back to the boat's interior, Jenna launched straight in.

As she related the conversation with Wallace Myers, Jenna gradually felt herself becoming split in two. Her voice sounded calm in her own ears. But her heart accelerated, her body tensed, like something at gut level registered far below conscious thought.

Initially, Noah's only response was to start down the steps. Moving slowly, concentrating on what she was saying.

Then it happened.

Jenna actually saw the light spark in his gaze. The intake of breath, the straightening of his entire body. She could even give his reaction a name.

Relief.

She forced herself to finish. Then stood there as a lump of ice congealed in her gut. Moving outward to consume her entire body. Making it hard to draw a decent breath.

Noah said, "Wallace's nerves come down to greed."

She heard herself say, "I thought that. At first." She puffed slightly. Like trying to talk after a hard race. "But I had the feeling there might be something else."

Noah frowned at the boat. "Like what?"

"I have no idea."

"Greed alone works well enough. Wallace is probably trying to gain from both sides of the deal. Keep a major slice of the proceeds for himself. He didn't tell you who the prospective buyer was, correct?"

"A Los Angeles attorney. Retired to a ranch north of Santa Barbara. Nothing more." Not even the day's heat could touch her. "You're not actually considering this."

"What's not to consider? If we push, we could probably up their offer to two and a half mil. And cut Wallace's share down to a straight commission."

"Noah. I won't . . . . No."

She might as well not have spoken. "After covering expenses we could clear three, maybe even four hundred thousand dollars. Each."

"I'm not interested."

"Jenna . . . There's two of us here. And I have final say."

The ice had a name now. Betrayal. She felt her thoughts and dreams congeal. She opened her mouth, but nothing emerged.

"I kept fifty-one percent, remember?"

She felt as though she faced the same silent lie as with Wallace. Noah scattered his gaze everywhere but directly at her. His voice held a false calm, like he said one thing and thought another. Which was when she realized.

This was not about the boat. At all.

It was about them. And her.

Noah saw this as an open door. A way out.

She found the strength to say, "So you'll do to me exactly what your former partner did to you."

Noah had the decency to wince. "This isn't the same."

"Oh, really."

"Not at all."

There wasn't any point in discussing this further. Why argue with a man who wanted to run away? Noah's attitude all week made perfect sense now.

Jenna forced herself to turn away. "Goodbye, Noah."

"Jenna, wait. We're not done."

She forced herself to keep moving. "That's precisely what I am, Noah. Done."

She found her car mostly by feel. The fractured vision at least kept her from seeing him clearly as she started the engine and reversed from the drive.

The valley road seemed endless. She tried her best to find consolation in how there had been no histrionics. No raised voices. No shattered glass. No rage or screams or any of the elements that had shaped her worst childhood memories.

Just the same, the moment was seismic.

Jenna stopped beyond the valley gates, just as soon as the farmhouse was no longer visible. As she struggled to regain control, she was struck by a very lonely thought.

So this was what it felt like to have a man make her cry.

CHAPTER 26

Five minutes later, an hour, Jenna had no concept of time's passage. Only that she was startled from her sad reverie by a tapping on her window. Jenna cleared her face, or tried to, and saw Amos standing there in a crisp clean uniform. Jenna opened her door and rose. She was very ashamed of her broken state, but the relief over being close to a caring friend was much stronger.

"I'd ask if everything was all right," Amos said, "but I don't like wasting my breath."

"Things are pretty awful," she confirmed.

He gestured to the empty highway. "Say the word, I'll be on my way. Pretend I didn't see you at all."

"No. Stay. Please. I need . . ." She took a deeply fractured breath. And told him.

As she spoke, Amos took off his hat and set it on the roof of her car. Next came his sunglasses, which he folded and inserted in his shirt pocket. Then he stood with arms folded, frowning into the western light. His position was almost identical to Noah's, and totally different.

158   *Davis Bunn*

When she was done, Amos said, "All this, it isn't about the boat."

The fact that someone saw this situation as she did caused Jenna to leak more tears. "No, it isn't."

"My brother is acting like ten kinds of fool." He kicked at a loose rock. "Unfortunately, being a total idiot isn't a felony in this county. But it should be."

"I don't know what to do."

He nodded agreement. "My wife would tell you that I don't know the first thing about relationships. But if you're wanting my advice . . ."

"Please."

"Give it a day or so. There's always hope Noah will realize he's in the wrong and come crawling back, begging for you to overlook the fact he should be locked up."

"Even if he did, I don't know if I can. Or should." She waved behind her, taking in the valley and the boat and everything. "If that's how he feels . . ."

She was halted by Amos shaking his head. "The thing is, our boy may be running from what isn't there anymore. You understand what I'm saying?"

"I think—"

"He's been burned bad. First the business was stolen, his lifelong dream taken by someone he trusted. Then his wife decides to kick him when he's down." Amos was nodding now, clearly liking the shape of these thoughts. "What I'm saying is, it might not be you at all."

She needed to wipe her face again. "I'll think about it."

"You do that."

She thought it was over. Time for him to go off on patrol and for her to go home and cope with just another empty night.

But as she started back for her car, Amos said, "You mind giving me the long version of what happened down in Morro Bay?"

So she went through her conversation with Wallace all over again. Hollowed by what happened next. But still liking how Amos took her seriously. Even when she said, "Noah thought it was just greed, how Wallace was acting."

"You don't agree."

"I don't have any reason not to. But no. I had the feeling there was something else at work. The man struck me as . . ."

"What?"

"Afraid." She had not mentally shaped the word until that very moment. Reliving the discussion had brought it to the fore. "Still, that doesn't mean Noah's wrong. Wallace could just have feared his biggest deal of the year might go south."

"Sure. Sure. But you don't think so."

"Tell you the truth, I don't know what I think."

Amos reached for his hat, touched her shoulder in the process. "Why don't you go relax. Give our buddy a chance to come to his senses and . . ."

It was the most natural thing in the world to embrace him. Tight as she could. Smell the clean shirt, feel the iron-hard man within. "Having you stop by kept my whole world from falling apart."

CHAPTER 27

Noah waited another two hours to make the call. There was no reason to delay contacting Wallace until so late in the afternoon. The salvage operator might already have been on the road. But after Jenna left, everything slowed.

Noah's every motion required such a huge effort. Like unseen weights were attached to his limbs, his heart, even his brain. The simplest task felt beyond him. Just crossing to his porch, climbing the stairs, going inside, finding his phone, calling Wallace.

Their conversation did not start well. And grew steadily worse.

"Hey, man. I was just on my way out the door."

"Don't come." Noah had to punch through an invisible fabric to shape each word. "There's no need for you to make the trip, because there's no deal."

"Wait, what? Jenna said . . ." Wallace went quiet. Like he shared Noah's need to reshape his world. When he came back, Wallace's voice had tensed. Like hands now gripped his throat. "I thought you guys were counting down to your last dime."

"You thought wrong."

"That's what you said. I heard you clear as day."

"Things change."

"Yeah, but see . . . I already told this guy—"

"What's his name?"

"Who?"

"Don't give me that. Your buyer. Who is he?"

"Look, he wants to hang back—"

"Then don't come." Noah found a need to steady himself by gripping the porch railing. "Here's how it's going to work. We agree on you receiving a finder's fee. Then you step away."

"No way, that's not—"

"I'm not finished. You are not, repeat not, part of any deal. The sale is straight from me to him. Setting the price, moving forward, all that happens without you being in-volved."

Everything he said, it all made perfect sense. Noah had handled dozens of such contracts. Hundreds. Attorneys and studio execs and directors and producers, all wanting to front the actual deal. Take a major cut, insert themselves into the decision-making process. His response was so cut-and-dry he could be reading from a script.

Only not this time.

Noah felt like each word he spoke added to the weight. Finally, he had no choice but to shift himself over, crossing the porch in vague shuffling steps, and let the nearest rocker take his full weight.

He half-listened to Wallace's whining response. The longer the man complained over how his guy wanted to stay in the background, the more certain Noah became. Jenna had been right all along. This wasn't just a salvage operator pushing for a bigger payday. There was a hint of desperation at work here. Bandsaw tension.

Gradually Wallace's voice receded into the distance.

Noah knew it wasn't actually happening. Just the same, the sensation was vivid. He felt like he was back in his dream. Only now he wasn't chasing after someone. Wallace might be moving through unseen rooms, drawing farther away. Noah remained there on his rear porch, staring at the barn and the boat. Wallace was the only one moving. The growing distance made room for the hollow void that now threatened to consume Noah.

He heard himself say, "This is new."

Wallace merely paused, like he couldn't be bothered to actually hear what Noah was saying. Then his bandsaw whine resumed. How it was time Noah accepted the boat for what it was, too big a project for just one man. Something he'd never finish. Especially not with his money nearly gone. And even if he did manage to get it back in the water, running costs on a boat this size . . .

Noah's voice was scarcely a whisper. The volume didn't matter, though. He was only talking to himself. "All this time, I've been looking in the wrong direction."

Wallace stopped. "Do you even hear what I'm telling you?"

Noah forced himself to take aim at the man on the phone. At least temporarily. "Your cut is five percent."

"No, but—"

"Don't call me unless it's to pass on the buyer's name."

Noah mostly cut the connection so he could focus on this new realization. It rose from somewhere deep, like a bubble moving slowly toward the surface of dark and troubled waters. Then it arrived in his conscious awareness, with a savage force that caused him to moan.

He'd been so focused on the past he couldn't see the *now*.

Jenna had been right all along. Not just about the boat. Or Wallace.

About everything.

Noah's burdens grew heavier with every passing minute. He sat there like an old man, hands dangling limp off the chair arms, head tilted back so the rocker took its weight. Another hour passed, or half an eternity, he couldn't tell which. Noah was mildly surprised the chair didn't collapse under its heavy load. His own weight, plus all the wrong moves and the guilt. All the bad thoughts and fears. Everything that had led him to hurt a good woman.

Because she cared for him.

He was still sitting there when Amos drove up and parked. Night had wrapped itself around the valley. He was sore and he was tired and hungry and getting colder by the minute. Noah's mind kept shooting out firefly sparks, half-formed thoughts that were shattered by the time they emerged. How it was growing cold. How he needed to shower off the day and get into clean clothes. Make something for dinner. Feed the dog and fill his water bowl.

Try to work out what he needed to say to Jenna.

Amos climbed the stairs and stood there, leaning against the railing. Arms crossed. Cutting a sharp and angry silhouette from the night. Silent. Waiting.

Shaping the words was almost more than Noah could bear. "I'm such a fool."

"No argument there."

Just the same, that simple exchange was enough to propel his brother into action. Amos entered the kitchen. There was the sound of running water, then of a shovel striking gravel. Amos emerged holding the pitcher and rubber bucket Noah used to feed Bear. He crossed the yard and spoke softly to the dog. Returned. Set the implements inside the kitchen.

Then, "Word to the wise. Don't go by my house just yet. It's hard to say who's madder at you just now, Aldana or my daughters. I've told them they're not allowed to shoot you on sight. But you know women."

Noah groaned. "They know."

"Well, of course. Seeing as how I needed to vent. Being so hot and all. And then Aldana called Ryan. I believe Zia's wife was also brought in on the discussion. Which means you've got three police and sheriff departments out for your sorry hide."

Noah asked, "What do I do now?"

"You want my advice, I'd say just hang tight."

"What's that supposed to mean?"

"What do you think?"

"Don't do anything. Wait."

"See, I knew you weren't as dumb as Aldana's been saying."

"That's going to be really, really hard."

"Aldana would tell you, hard is exactly what you deserve." Amos walked over, stood there a long moment, then kicked the rocker's base. "Enough. Get on inside, shower off the day. I'll fix you something to eat. We'll talk our way through this mess." When Noah didn't move, Amos kicked harder. "That was an order, recruit."

CHAPTER 28

Jenna picked at an early dinner, tried to watch television, failed at reading a book, then gave up on the day. She went through the motions of preparing for bed—lay down, cut off the light, and stared at the ceiling. Images from the conversations flashed with cinematic clarity. The day's events left her feeling like Noah had punctured her heart and all the life-force had been expelled. She heard him discuss selling the boat with that deadly calm. Impatiently she wiped her face on the edge of her sheet and turned over. She wished she knew what to do.

It seemed as though a few breaths passed, not longer. Then the phone chimed. When she opened her eyes, it was to sunlight glaring through the east-facing window. She had not bothered to close the drapes, since she knew she wouldn't sleep.

She settled her feet on the carpet, rubbed her face, then picked up the phone and saw it was Amos. Calling her at 9:19 in the morning. "Amos?"

"We're across the street. And we'll stay right here unless you give us the word."

Her heart skipped a beat. "We?"

"Zia and I. He's got something I think you should hear."

She was mildly angry with herself, how disappointed she felt that it wasn't Noah. Then she pushed it away, classing it as a momentary lapse, down to still being barely awake. "Give me ten minutes," she said. "Then come on up."

She was showered and dressed and making breakfast when they knocked on her open door. Amos called, "Jenna?"

"In the kitchen." She smiled a welcome and kept slicing peaches into a bowl. Jenna pointed to three mugs and a pitcher and sugar bowl stationed by the coffee maker. "Help yourself."

"Don't want to take too much of your time, coming in unexpected like this."

"I'm glad you're here." She saw how Amos studied her for visible cracks. How Zia remained vaguely ashamed. It was the first time she had seen the San Lu detective since the agent had come probing. "Want some breakfast?"

"What are you making there?"

"Plain Greek-style yogurt. Peaches, berries, a sprinkling of granola. Breakfast of champions."

"Make that a pair of egg and chorizo burritos," Zia said. "Maybe a cerveza, I'll be interested."

"Something about a lady offering me a too-healthy meal brings tears to my eyes," Amos said.

"Liar."

"Tell the truth, your breakfast takes me straight back to Aldana's tofu diet phase. Made it herself, these big square pans of fresh baby barf."

She spooned in blackberries. "I bet you ate it and loved it."

"I pretended to. Anything for a happy home. But me and the girls took to eating out one square meal every day."

"You fellows want to move into the dining room?"

"Here's fine." Amos took a solemn pull from his mug, then, "How are you holding up?"

"Good, now that you're here." She leaned against the counter, ate a spoonful. The two men managed to compress the kitchen's air. All the bitter regrets had been expelled. Leaving Jenna able to breathe easy. "Otherwise, the day would probably be touch and go."

"Aldana said to tell you, we've got an empty guest room. She and the girls are ready to help you chase ghosts."

"Thank them for me, but I think I'll avoid the valley for a while."

Amos started to say something, then shifted gears and used his mug to gesture at Zia. "My buddy's got some news."

"It's about the old man," Zia said.

"He means the late great Dino or whoever he was."

"The lady knows exactly who I'm in referral."

"That isn't actually a sentence."

"You bring me here to criticize my diction?"

"Or something."

Jenna knew the grousing was at least partly intended to put her and them both at ease. Play the jesters to lighten their arrival in a bad hour. As she ate and listened, she observed something more, an internal state they had banished. The morning that she would not be having. Lying in her lonely bed, having little or no motivation to move.

Sooner or later she was going to have to face the day, and all the ones to follow. As she ate and watched them bicker, Jenna was momentarily tempted to contact Sol, tell him to arrange a new patient. But just as swiftly, she expelled the thought. She had no interest in running away. She had spent all these years moving *toward* the inherited dream. She needed to treat this as a momentary setback. Nothing more.

Then a sudden welling of regret threatened to stain the hour. Jenna pushed at it hard as she could, swallowed a lump of something far rougher than her breakfast, and said, "Guys, look. Whatever the news you're dancing around, it's okay. Dino has more or less been filed in the past-tense drawer. So out with it. Please."

Zia took a step away from his friend. "Okay, so not all fibbies are a bad smell like mister super-Anglo."

Amos said, "He means the agent with three first names."

"Give it a rest. She knows." To Jenna, "I spoke with a pal in DC. He used to be AIC for the central California office. We worked on a couple of big cases together. He's definitely one of the good guys."

Amos said, "He means Agent in Charge."

"Right. So sixty years ago, your Dino was accountant to the Chicago Mob."

Suddenly there was no room in the day for remorse. "He thinks or he knows?"

"My pal was definite. Benny Watts was the numbers guy responsible for turning bad money into semi-legal tender."

Jenna protested, "But that was a different era."

"Exactly what I told my buddy. Know what he said?"

"I have no idea whatsoever."

Zia clearly enjoyed his moment in the spotlight. "Maybe you should be sitting down."

"I'm not moving an inch. Tell me."

"What he said was, making off with a hundred mil of the Mob's money makes him a person of interest for a lot longer than that."

She breathed. Again. "Dino stole a hundred million dollars."

Zia said, "My pal said that was the absolute minimum."

Amos was grinning now. "Remember, we're talking early sixties. Back when a hundred million dollars was real money."

She laughed. It felt so good, so cleansing, she did it again. "Back in the day."

"There you go. Anyway, my pal checked the old files. The Mob was never sure it was Benny who took their money."

"Call him Dino. Please."

Zia nodded. "Apparently your guy was responsible for laundering their cash and putting it into legitimate businesses. Casinos, hotels, office buildings, a lot of what then was the new Chicago waterfront. The Mob bosses, they loved the guy."

Jenna set her bowl in the sink, surprised to see she had eaten everything. Then she slid over to make herself a mug. "This sounds so like Dino. I can almost see him smiling."

"Stealing a hundred mil from the Mob," Amos said. "I wish I had known him."

"I wish I had *arrested* the guy," Zia said.

Amos said, "Then one day . . ."

"The guy vanishes," Zia said, enjoying the exchange now. "Plays like smoke in the wind. Poof and gone."

"So the Mob brings in a new accountant."

"Right. And this new fellow, he starts going through Benny's books . . ."

Amos was chuckling now. "And he says . . ."

"Sorry to tell you, but hey, these numbers, they don't add up." Zia grinned.

"So the Mob . . ."

"Like kicking over an ant hill."

Amos looked at Jenna, eyes merry. "Scrambling like mad. Searching everywhere."

Jenna asked, "When did Dino appear in Santa Barbara?"

"There you go." Zia nodded. "Eleven years later. First record of him. Buys the house in the hills. Applies for a California driver's license. Registers to vote. Puts down 'retired' as his profession."

"Was he married?"

"Yes, to Dorothy. Shows up in Santa Barbara with wife

and one daughter, Eloise. Then his wife died in childbirth fourteen months later. Dino never remarried."

"Just a retired guy living small," Amos said. "Never gets arrested. Never has any reason to have his fingerprints taken. Lives a quiet and law-abiding life to the end."

"This is wild," Jenna said.

"What I said to my pal. Exactly."

Amos asked, "What happened between him leaving Chicago and arriving here?"

Zia shook his head. "Nobody knows."

"So he lays low somewhere until he can pretend to be this new guy." Amos asked Jenna, "He never mentioned his own parents?"

"Just his dad, just the one time. He died when Dino was twelve. Apparently he worked for the Chicago Mob."

Zia and Amos shared a look. "Interesting."

She thought back. "As for his wife, I didn't even know her name until now. Like I said, the man was a closed book."

"So Dino Vicenza is a retired widower, raising two daughters on his own. He plants himself in a nice quiet central California town." Amos shook his head. "Definitely one for the books."

Jenna recalled moments when the nice old man, her friend, revealed shadows of a dark side. The sudden rages, all out of proportion to the situation, or so it seemed to her. At the time, she had simply put it down to Dino having a bad day. But now she could link them together under a new heading. These were remnants of who Dino had once been. A truly bad man. A mobster. A thief.

Just the same, she had grown to like him. Knowing his past didn't change that. Even if perhaps it should.

Jenna realized they were watching her. "Like I said. I've never met anyone who loved secrets more than Dino."

"No surprise there," Zia said. "He had a hundred million reasons to keep it that way."

Jenna walked the two men back to their respective rides. They stood there in the day's growing heat, until Amos told his friend, "Go ahead and give her the other half."

Zia said, "We heard about, you know."

"He means Noah acting like a total dodo."

"There's no law against a man playing stupid," Zia said. "Else we'd all be behind bars."

Amos huffed. "Maybe you would."

Zia snorted. "Oh, and now you're Mister Perfection." To Jenna, "Me and some buddies, we've been saving for years. Planning to buy us a boat. We'd all like to go in together, buy shares."

Amos said, "My Aldana says we want to be part of this too."

Zia said, "This from the man who gets seasick looking at pictures of boats in magazines."

"Long as I can choose the right days for my trips," Amos said, "I'll do fine."

Jenna fought down the sudden urge to hug them both. Weep. Something. "Guys, I can't tell you what this means. But Noah owns fifty-one percent."

"My brother is not selling his share to anybody without your approval," Amos said. "He just doesn't know it yet."

This time, Zia's grin held a cop's steely glint. "Me and the boys, we'll escort Amos's idiot brother somewhere empty and quiet. Keep him there until the situation is totally elucidated."

"Illuminated," Amos said. "I have no earthly idea what you mean by that last comment. And I don't want to know."

Jenna reached out. Finding great comfort in gripping them both. "I don't know what to say."

They stood there for a long moment, Jenna as close to

happy as she'd been in a while. Finally, Amos said to Zia, "Why don't you take on off, let me and the lady have a word."

"Whatever you need," Zia told her. "Whenever. Just let me know."

"You took the words right out of my mouth," Jenna replied. "And my heart."

Amos waited until Zia drove away to say, "I don't know how you feel about giving my brother another chance. Truth be told, Aldana isn't sure he deserves anything but a bullet at sunrise."

She pressed a fist to her stomach. Doing her best to keep her breakfast down. "Tell me."

"Noah is beyond sorry. He knows he made a terrible mistake." Amos took his time, staring down the empty road. "Aldana likes to say that good women are born knowing their men will get things totally wrong, fall on their faces, whatever. She brings that up a lot when I deserve worse than she gives me."

Jenna knew she needed to say something. About how Amos was one of the finest people she had ever known. How much it meant to call him a friend. But just then it was hard to take a simple breath.

Amos went on. "Aldana says the answer to two questions make all the difference. First, will they admit they're wrong, and be ready to grow beyond their mistakes. And second, will they apologize."

"That's three questions, not two."

"Three parts, two questions. This according to Aldana." Amos focused on her. "Then comes the hard part."

Jenna did not respond.

"Deciding whether it's worth the time, trouble, and future pain to accept the apology. And move on."

She remained silent.

"What I'm trying to say is, if women didn't have this forgiveness index in their genes, humanity would have gone extinct long ago."

"Forgiveness index."

"Aldana's words."

"I like it."

"She is one smart woman. And forgiving."

Jenna understood what Amos was not saying. The man was making his request, or invitation, whatever. Clear as day. Saying this was the path he thought she should take.

The queasy tightness to her middle left as abruptly as it had come. Leaving her slightly weightless. Able to release the hand on her gut, able to say what she was thinking. "When Noah was telling me about what happened to his business, his dream, he said he thought he'd have more time. It resonated. I've heard that from any number of my patients."

Amos nodded. "I expect I'll be feeling some of that myself, when my own final hour comes."

"I almost never think about patients once they, you know."

"Once they've punched their ticket. I expect that's a healthy perspective."

"Maybe so, but last night I saw them. One after the other. Speaking those words. How they thought there would be more time. Feeling their regret. Their sense of guilt."

"I don't like the sound of that word. *Guilt.*"

"Guilt," Jenna repeated. "Not using the time well, not taking the chance, whatever. They're reaching out of the dark and they're warning me. Telling me not to make their mistake. Be sure and take the time. Don't put off life. Or love. Live each day to the fullest. Count the minutes given to joy as a triumph."

She found it necessary to stop then. Breathe around the ache. The sorrow. The fear.

When she looked up, she saw Amos watching her. His obsidian features softened and open. He asked, "Is that a yes?"

She nodded. "Tell Noah he's welcome to call."

CHAPTER 29

Later that afternoon, Noah called.

She listened to his apology in silence. In truth, she did not take in the words. They formed a gentle wash, dousing her injured heart and spirit. When he was done, she thanked him solemnly. He asked if he could see her. She replied from some great distance, saying they should speak again the next morning. He responded with a silence that Jenna found suitable. He sighed an acceptance. And murmured a farewell.

Afterward she sat in her living room, examining her internal state. Trying to work out how she felt. Wondering what she wanted to happen next.

She went through what used to be her normal routine. Back when she returned home from another patient. Back before the boat and Noah entered her life. She drove into town. Walked the central avenue. Shopped for fresh veggies and fruit. Came home. Boiled eggs. Sliced avocado and garden tomato. Grilled a minute steak. Ate a warm salad. Pretended to be interested in a show. Fielded a few texts and emails. Went to bed. To her surprise, she slept well and did not dream.

The next morning Noah called again.

This time was slightly different, in that he had a specific request. Wanting her to drive out, take part in a first meeting with Wallace and the mystery buyer.

Jenna listened to him in silence. In truth, she had no issue with Noah's request. Of course she would help him. This was not really what interested her, not at the level of bone and sinew. Her attention was fastened upon something else. Noah was the one who was uncertain now. Clearly worrying over whether Jenna would allow him back inside her heart and her world. Or if the new boundaries remained. Friends with very tight borders, keeping the other at arm's length. Because she said so.

She reveled in not needing to decide. Taking time to breathe through the pain he had caused her. Allowing it to slowly begin to dissolve and fade.

She felt as though the moment held the same sort of necessary distance as other times when she returned home. Enduring the impossible, one patient at a time. Then healing and moving on.

Just like now.

"Let me make sure I get this right," she said once he was finished and silent. "You want me to sit in while you dicker with a buyer who is not, repeat not, getting our boat?"

"Sort of, yeah."

"Why not just tell him no and be done with it?"

"Sure, I can do that. I will, if that's what you want."

She let the silence linger. Tasting what it meant to have the power to decide. Listening to that internal chorus. *Balance.* "You think it's important we do this."

"What I think is, you may have been right about Wallace being after more than just a bigger percentage."

"He was pushing because he had to."

"Motive," Noah agreed. "We need to have a better grasp of what's actually happening here."

"Maybe you should handle this by yourself. They see you as the boat's sole owner."

"Jenna, no. I need you." He stopped. "If that sounded totally desperate, it's because I am."

"Actually, I thought it sounded nice."

"You did?" The words carried more than a hint of desperation. "Jenna. Please, I need you."

She listened to the silence and the echo of his sad hopefulness. Felt remnants of her own sorrow. Then, "Make the call. Text and let me know when I should come out."

"Come now," he replied. "This very instant."

"Noah . . ."

"Yes. All right." Resigned. "Bye."

CHAPTER 30

When Jenna arrived that afternoon, Noah felt such overwhelming relief he wanted to give it physical form. Drop to his knees, weep, something. For the first time ever he felt a kinship to earlier generations. People who marked transitional events by offering sacrifices to unseen powers.

Just the same, the moment was far from perfect.

Noah made them coffee and then joined her in the farmhouse's kitchen. The round-shouldered refrigerator hummed a steady note. The battered table matched the raw-wood flooring, the worn and weary sink and Bakelite stove.

Jenna cradled a mug whose floral arrangement had been reduced to pastel shadows. She sipped thoughtfully and listened as he struggled through yet another apology.

When Wallace showed up twenty minutes later, it was by way of a Mercedes S-Class, the limo version that cost over a hundred and fifty thou new. A uniformed driver remained at the wheel, barely visible through the darkened windshield.

The two made quite a pair. Wallace topped out at five-ten, a human fireplug with reddish-gray Brillo-style curls on his head and chest and arms. Dressed as usual in ratty shorts, salt-encrusted boat shoes, and a vintage T-shirt.

The man who accompanied him was something else entirely.

Lane Pritchard was tall and narrow and moved like an aging waterbird, picking up each foot and planting it carefully. He wore tan Italian loafers and socks the color of old cream. The ivory pants and yellow knit shirt might as well have been selected to accent his pale skin. Round tortoise-shell sunglasses masked his gaze. A gold Rolex rattled on his bony wrist.

Noah could not imagine anybody much further removed from his idea of a boat guy.

Lane's handshake was a surprise. Iron hard, tight as a noose. "Mr. Hearst, a genuine pleasure. I've heard such good things."

Noah waited until the guy let him have his hand back. "That right? Who from?"

"Well, Wallace of course. He thinks the world of you and your craftsmanship. But we also share a number of common acquaintances. I did considerable business with several of your former clients."

"That a fact. Which ones?"

Lane tch-tched. Like Noah had stepped over the line and entered some legal gray zone. "I never mention names, Mr. Hearst. Many of my clients prefer it that way."

"Wallace said something about you being retired."

"That's partly correct. I no longer take on new clients. But if an old associate insists on my serving their interests, who am I to argue?"

Noah glanced at the shorter man. Wallace stood two steps back, remaining as still as a frightened rodent. Waiting to see which way to jump. "Wallace had it wrong, didn't he?"

"Excuse me?"

"The boat's not for you at all."

"Well, yes and no. Several of my oldest clients and friends love the open water. All this is new to me, but I'm learning to share their passion. Which brings us to the point. I and my associates are interested in acquiring your craft."

"Sorry. I've had time to think things through. And I've decided the boat's not for sale."

Lane Pritchard turned slowly, focusing on Wallace. The boatyard operator whined, "You're running out of money. You said so yourself."

"I was. Yes."

Lane held Wallace with his hidden gaze. "And now?"

"A group of buddies are chipping in, buying shares of my boat."

"Even so, running costs on such a craft must be astronomical."

"Probably. Which is why it's good to have friends involved. Speaking of which, I'm happy to sell you shares. A hundred and fifty thou. Each."

"How many shares are there?"

"Thirty," Noah replied, making it up as he went along. "Twenty-eight are already taken. Same goes for you, Wallace. Long as you don't try to rent it out to anyone else. That's written into the share certificates. Use of the boat is not transferable."

Lane studied the heavily perspiring Wallace for a moment longer, then turned and offered Noah a meaningless smile. "In that case, I believe I've taken enough of your time."

"Is that a no on the share offer?"

"I'll need to speak with my associates. Can you give me a day?"

"Take three. You too, Wallace." He waved at the shadows holding the boat. "Why don't you let me show you around?"

"Tempting as that sounds, I'd rather wait until I speak with my clients." When he glanced at Wallace, the man responded with a tight shudder. "It's time we were going."

Noah offered his hand. "Always a pleasure to talk shop with a fellow boat guy."

Jenna waited until the dark-windowed Mercedes started back down the valley road to descend from the porch. She stood beside him and watched the car write a dusty script into the pale-blue sky. "I can't decide which guy creeps me out more."

In response, Noah started for the house. It felt better than good to have a renewed sense of purpose. "I need to make a call."

CHAPTER 31

Noah grabbed his phone from the kitchen, asked, "You want a coffee or something?"

"I want you to tell me what is going on."

He walked back, seated himself, cradled the phone, all the while studying her. The sun-flushed features, the strong limbs, the easy manner, this silent intensity. The realization of how close he had come to losing it all, how much he deserved nothing less, left him breathless and aching.

She asked, "What?"

"I'm so very, very sorry."

The sunlight showed deep in her gaze. Gold flecks, green diamonds, watching. She asked, "Who are you calling?"

"Her name is Lorna Chase. She's served as my attorney since before I started my company . . ."

She waited with him, then pressed, "Why does that make you sad?"

"She was a friend. I haven't contacted her since it all went south."

Jenna seemed able to read the invisible script. "She handled your divorce?"

"She did, yes."

"And the sale of your company." It was not a question.

"The theft," he corrected. "That too."

"If this lady is truly your friend, she will understand why you haven't been in touch." Jenna pointed at his phone. "Make the call."

Lorna's secretary kept him waiting only a few minutes. When his former attorney came on the line, she greeted him with, "I was hoping you'd call. Not turn into another of those ghosts of failed clients that litter my bad nights."

"You didn't fail at anything," Noah replied. The phone was set on the rickety porch table, with their chairs to either side. "Not with me. And I'm sorry I haven't been in touch."

Lorna Chase had always reminded Noah of a strict schoolteacher. The precise diction, the kindly no-nonsense way of dealing with clients, the sharply intelligent manner used to cutting egos down to size. Lorna had negotiated the freelance contract with a small indie producer that had served as the springboard for Noah going out on his own. She had handled the sale of his company and his divorce. And taken both personally. "No apologies necessary. How are you, Noah?"

He resisted the urge to check Jenna's expression for the right answer. "Adjusting. Healing. Slowly."

"I'm glad. You deserved far better than I was able to get for you."

"You did ten times better than anyone else, a hundred times better than I feared."

"Yes. Well. Nice of you to say."

"I'm here with Jenna Greaves. She and I are partners on a boat project."

"Are you really. How is that going?"

This time, Noah looked over. Jenna kept her gaze on the phone and gave him nothing more than her standard calm. "I'm learning a lot. Mostly about myself. Making mistakes along the way. Trying to grow from them. Correct what I can."

"Sounds like a healing is in the works."

"I hope so. Look, I'm calling because an LA lawyer is interested in buying our boat. I was hoping you could give us a handle on him."

"You do realize LA has more lawyers than wannabe starlets."

"He claims to have come across my work, representing unnamed clients. Which means he's been involved at least peripherally in the film world."

"Okay, that narrows things. What's his name?"

"Lane Pritchard."

Silence.

"Hello?"

Lorna's voice dropped a full octave. "Lane Pritchard wants to buy your boat."

"Drove up today. Claims he wants to make us a cash offer."

"Must be some boat."

"Eighty-four feet. Bought at police auction after it was severely damaged and sunk. Putting it back together has been keeping us busy."

"Did you agree to the sale?"

When she looked up, Noah met Jenna's gaze. "No, Lorna. We're not."

Another silence. Then, "I really can't help you, Noah. Sorry."

The rocker creaked as he leaned forward. Opened his mouth. Searched for what to say. Tried to remember when Lorna had responded to a request of his with flat denial. Came up blank.

Lorna went on. "It's best if you do not contact our *law of-fices* again. *Especially* regarding the sale of a boat. *Any* boat."

"I don't . . ."

"*My firm* is unable to represent you in any such matters. Goodbye."

When the call ended, Jenna asked, "What just happened?"

Noah leaned back. Rocked.

"Noah?"

He reached out. "Can I borrow your phone?"

But as he started to dial Lorna's private number on Jenna's phone, Noah was struck by a realization. Straight to the heart, hard as an iron fist.

He had recognized it from the beginning, of course, how different she was from everything that had come before. Jenna's unique nature had always been there.

But for the first time Noah accepted the very real challenge, precisely what it meant, to *let the past go.*

For this to work, for them to have any hope of a future together, he had to stop viewing this amazing woman through the lens of yesterday.

All the fears and pains and bad moves caused by other people. They had nothing to do with Jenna.

And his misplaced perspective had almost cost him everything.

At least, everything that mattered.

He asked Jenna, "Is it too late?"

She watched him. Gaze unblinking, steady.

"I mean, for us."

"I know what you mean." She studied him. "I hope not."

Noah huffed a hard breath. Could not think of any adequate response. His hand shook slightly as he coded in the number.

*　*　*

Lorna's phone rang once, then, "Noah?"

"Yes."

"Whose phone is this?"

"Jenna Greaves."

"Your partner, right?"

He ducked his head with shame. "Yes."

"Tell me exactly how this has happened."

Noah gave it to her in careful stages. Jenna watched him in her singular fashion, wide-eyed, fully alert, very still.

A few moments later, Lorna replied, "It's entirely possible that I'm being overly cautious. But until this situation is resolved, any further contact between us needs to be done with great care."

"Can you tell me why?"

"If the situation escalates, if this is about more than just a boat, you need to assume legal niceties will not stop these people from doing whatever they feel is in their best interests. Including tapping phones. Breaching attorney-client privilege. And so on."

"Okay, now I'm worried."

"Perhaps you should be. Several of my clients are independent producers. Among this group, Lane Pritchard is known as a lender of last resort. As in, only go to him when all other options are exhausted. And even then, it's probably best to let the project go. Bankruptcy might actually be a better alternative. Nothing has ever managed to stick, but Lane has been brought up three times before the California Bar for what amounts to illegalities. He's known as a shadow figure. Everything else I say is conjecture. Are you sure you want to hear?"

"Absolutely."

"There have been rumors that Hollywood has become a good option for laundering drug money. The producer's accounts show a small investment from some fund that Pritchard represents. In return, they receive an overlarge percentage of the final product. This visible investment, the legal money, does not justify the size of their share in the project. You understand?"

"The rest is under the table."

"Right. But problems arise when the films do not earn back. Producers find themselves handing over percentages of all future projects. In some cases, they lose their companies, their homes, the works. In other cases . . ."

"Tell us."

"They just vanish. One of them was a client. I tried to find out where she had gone. That was the one time I met Lane. He just happened to be standing outside a courtroom when I finished a case. Lane said it would be best if I let the matter drop. Then he walked away."

Jenna spoke for the first time. "He came with Wallace Myers, the boatyard owner we've been using for repairs. Apparently Wallace had told Lane the sale was a real possibility. When Noah said otherwise, Wallace became genuinely terrified. The look Lane gave him, it was like seeing an assassin's blade."

"There you go," Lorna said. "If you want my opinion, Lane Pritchard is a stone-cold killer. He might not pull the trigger. But he's good at his job. And what's more, he enjoys it."

CHAPTER 32

Jenna left soon after. She asked Noah not to respond to Lane's offer for a while, give her time to think. Invited him to stop by the next day for a coffee. They set the time, or rather, she suggested ten and he responded with a beggar's gratitude.

She went through the motions of just another day. Wondering at herself and this distance she felt was now so necessary. He had done precisely what she wanted. And she responded with holding him at arm's length. Jenna had no idea why, only that she needed to understand this internal state before taking any next step.

The next morning, half past nine, there he was. Seated on the same bench in the little park. Like he had been planted there. Like he would wait all day if necessary. For her.

Jenna took her time. She wasn't waiting because she still needed to decide what she wanted to have happen. She was too long a realist to play games with her heart.

She loved this man. So much.

Just the same, she needed something to happen. That was

all she had come up with during the night. A reassurance that they were moving beyond the situation that had fractured her world. A clear sense that this would not happen again. That Noah's two-step was finished. That they could move forward into whatever came next. Together.

When she felt as ready as she was ever going to be, she left her apartment, crossed the parking area, walked through the gates, and watched him rise to his feet. Noah looked as nervous as she felt. Even more so.

She kissed his cheek and said, "Why don't you come inside."

Watching Noah enter her home and make a slow circuit, Jenna saw her apartment from a completely different perspective. The high-ceilinged rooms, the prints of favorite Impressionists on her walls, the neat and orderly manner in which she had shaped her haven from the world. Then, "This is so beautiful. It suits you."

She brought him into the kitchen, put on a fresh pot of coffee, and waited.

Noah took that as his cue. "I've spent these hours trying to figure out what I should say. How I can move beyond just another apology. Beg for another chance. All that I've already said."

"And?"

"I have no idea. Nothing I've come up with even holds a candle to how I feel."

She poured them both a mug. Added milk to her own. Took a step away from where he stood. Said what had come to mind when she'd seen him waiting. For her.

"Growing up, I had these times when I felt no one would ever be there for me. My mother was in the next room, locked in battles she fought by herself, a war she'd never win. I was certain she couldn't even see me. As far as she was concerned, I just reflected the man who had robbed her of the future she thought she deserved." Jenna watched Noah's unsteady hand as he plied the milk pitcher. Watched him use both hands to take a sip. "I've spent most of my life being framed by this sense of not belonging. Doing what I could for others, so they wouldn't end their lives the way mine had begun. It's only now, over these past couple of days, that I've seen how much this solitude has come to dominate my world. Shaped my perspective. Kept me adrift. And alone."

Noah might have nodded.

She said, "Now it's your turn."

His words emerged in a soft, steady beat. Like they were timed to a verbal metronome. Counting out the lost minutes. "I've spent these days looking back over our time together. I've had these incredible moments when I've seen you clearly. Just for a few seconds. Realize what a truly amazing woman you are. Then my past would drop like a veil. And I'd get so scared." He showed her that raw and open gaze. "I'm scared now. Terrified. I have no idea what to do. Just the same, I know . . ."

"Tell me."

"I want us to be together." The words became slightly fractured, like he struggled against some internal quake. "I want to be good enough to deserve you."

Noah's desperate urgency pushed her into the same protective bubble she maintained around patients. Keeping her safe regardless of what crisis she faced.

She wondered at this. How love had brought her to the point where she was again facing the same impossible situation she had experienced with her patients. And just like then, she did not have the answers.

But having the answers was not the issue. Not really.

What she could do was help Noah find his own way forward.

She nodded, a fractional move; most of it was internal. Feeling harmony with the thoughts as they took form. She knew what to do. The question was, how would he respond? Because this wasn't just about giving Noah her heart.

She needed to know if he was truly ready to take himself, and their relationship, to the next level.

Open himself up to a new tomorrow. One where Noah did as he said he wanted, and saw her for who she was. Without yesterday's veil forming a divider between them.

Soon as her decision took shape, Jenna knew what she was going to say.

"My favorite professor in my master's program talked about the brain's flexibility. The example he used came from surgeries to remove severe cataracts. These barriers to good vision don't develop in one fell swoop. It takes time. Months, sometimes years. Often the transition is gradual, the patient can pretend it isn't happening, until there is an event. Perhaps they discover one day they can't read a book anymore. Or they don't recognize their own child. Something. The reason why they're able to ignore this transition is because the brain is constantly recalibrating. Adjusting to the external situation. Interpreting whatever the senses are able to offer."

She could see Noah was confused by this. He wanted to ask where she was going. But fear held him back. Jenna took her time, holding to her internal state. *She was in control.* This was her choice, her next step. This was a new kind of liberty.

She went on. "After cataract surgery, the patient *can't see.* Going from their previous long-term blurred state to clarity means the brain has to recalibrate. The incoming sensual data is unfamiliar. The mind needs to relearn how to filter things out. This process is a very real shock. Often the patient is terrified by what is required."

Noah scarcely breathed the words. "I think I understand."

She resisted the urge to hug him. The intensity of being close with this man, the hope that things might truly enter a new phase, forced her to stop. Take a breath. Then she continued. "The patients I dealt with faced this same situation, only in reverse. Age and infirmity meant that in most cases, they *resisted* change. They were as terrified of it as they were of death. Sometimes more so. Control was stripped away. The daily decline was one step further along a road they had no choice but travel. This defined the second part of my job. Of course my primary task was to ease their final transition. But to be a true friend in these last hours, I needed to help them deal with change. And with fear."

He took his time. Spaced out the words. "I really, really want your help, Jenna. I *need* it."

"All right."

He swung completely around, so as to face her, his right knee now pressing against her. "Really?"

"Yes, Noah. If you're absolutely certain."

"I could not be more so." He took a long breath. "About the boat. I want you to have the two percent. Have control of what we do. Become the primary decision maker."

She could see the next step as clearly as if the words were scripted in the air before her face. "I think we should meet with Amos."

"I . . . What?"

"And Zia. And Ethan. And their wives. All of us together."

Noah squinted in confusion. "Can I ask why?"

"Of course." She told him what her idea was. Heard the matter-of-fact way she spoke. But in truth, her heart raced like a bird seeking to escape its cage. She was not merely making a suggestion for how they should proceed. This was not about the boat. Not really. It never had been. Just the same, the boat was a huge part of whatever happened next. For them. The couple named Jenna and Noah.

When she finished, she leaned against the counter, sipped from her mug, and waited. Glad she had done it. She wasn't nearly as certain about what she had said as it probably had sounded. But she knew it was the right step. A very strange certainty filled her. What she was doing, at its deepest level, was moving forward. Showing Noah what it meant to share control. Allow her to name the next step. Even when it was utterly, totally different from what he himself probably wanted.

Finally, he said, "I agree with you."

"Are you sure? Because there's no way you can take this back."

"Yes, Jenna. This is right. More than that. It's what I should have thought of on my own." When she did not respond, he went on. "The boat is one small part of a much bigger issue. No, small doesn't fit. I'm talking about us. About love. About being a couple together. It terrifies me to say those words. But it's true."

Jenna set down her mug, walked forward, took hold of his arm, and guided him out of the kitchen. Willing herself forward, before she gave in to the desire to hold him and just not let go. For this wiser side, the one who actually seemed to know how to handle things, said, *Not yet*. She opened her front door and said, "Thank you for coming today, Noah."

"Is that a yes?"

"It is me saying I need some more time." She allowed herself to embrace him. Ever so briefly. Forced herself to step back, let him go. "Let me know when we're going to meet with the others."

CHAPTER 33

Noah stopped on the way home and picked up takeaway Chinese, enough for lunch and dinner both. He had not eaten breakfast, and picked at the previous evening's meal. Noah had not actually finished a decent meal since Jenna had walked out of his life. Or rather, since he had forced her away.

For the first time since Amos had brought over the dog, neither daughter showed up to take Bear for his sunset walk. There could have been no clearer message, what Aldana and her daughters thought of him. Noah had made himself a pariah.

After eating his solitary meal, he took Bear for a long walk, climbing the scarred ridge and following the hillside path until he was exhausted enough to make what he knew were going to be three awful calls.

He received three identical responses. Each time, they must have seen who was calling, because they all answered with voices flat and hard. "Yes."

"This is Noah."

Their view of what he'd done, the attitude they took toward him now, was immediately evident. By the third call, which was to Zia, enduring their silent response should have been easier to take. It wasn't.

"Jenna asks if we can all meet."

"She'll be there?"

"She will. Yes."

"What time?"

"Would eleven tomorrow morning work for you? And can you please bring . . . Hello? Zia?"

Dawn the next morning found Noah already outside working on his boat. In the past, he had lived for his work. Now it was what kept him intact. He refused to give in to the desire to stop and stand and worry and hope. He feared any moment of inaction would render him permanently stuck. Seasons might come and go, he would remain just another mute statue, lifeless and stained by storms of his own making. When it was time, he went inside, showered, forced himself to eat a meal he didn't taste, put on a fresh pot of coffee, then stood on the rear porch. Waiting. Alone.

They all arrived early. Everyone was there and settled twenty minutes before Jenna was due. Noah greeted them solemnly as they climbed the rear stairs and settled on the porch, where they could look back over the boat. And scald him with gazes that arrested, convicted, and sentenced. Including the wives. Seven of them seated there, waiting for the lady of the hour. They remained distinctly separate, and not just from Noah. Their feelings about him and his actions had fragmented this group. He suspected they were waiting for him to try to apologize before launching in. Especially Aldana, who simmered by her husband, ready to explode.

Then Jenna pulled up. Noah went over to greet her, and

followed her back up the steps, settled her in the last rocker, went inside for a straight-backed kitchen chair, then stood there. Cleared his throat. "If I may say something."

"It better be good," Aldana snapped. "For your sake. So good you need to say it on your knees."

"If I thought it would help, I would," Noah said. "I've apologized to her. I want to do the same to all of you."

They responded with a unified silence.

"Just so you know, I offered Jenna the two percent that gives her full control over the boat."

"You should've done that at the beginning." Aldana glanced at the others. "Somebody tell me I'm wrong."

Despite their evident anger, and Jenna's silence, Noah had the distinct sense of having turned a corner. Despite his mistakes. Despite everything. They were, and would remain, his friends. He had no reason to feel his world was intact again. Just the same, he felt it was time to seat himself. Join the group. And say, "I've been fighting old battles."

"Shadowboxing with old ghosts," Amos said. "I've done that myself from time to time."

"Don't you let him off easy," Aldana told her husband. "Don't you dare."

"Who said anything about letting him off? But what he just said, what he's seeing, you got to admit it's a step in the right direction."

Aldana smoldered, then, "Okay, maybe a teeny tiny one."

Noah said, "The temptation to see today through the lens of yesterday is almost too great. Which is why I want Jenna to take over the controlling interest."

Aldana demanded, "You better not be talking just about that boat."

"No, I'm not."

Which was when Jenna reached over and took his hand. The act was so natural, so unexpected, he struggled to take it in. He stared at her fingers in his and decided this was what it felt like to hope again. This was the reality of a second chance.

Jenna said, "Noah and I have talked things over."

"Mostly she talked and I listened," Noah said. "After I got the apology out of the way."

Aldana snorted. "You don't get off that easy, mister. This apology of yours, we're talking years."

Noah looked at the hand holding his. "Yes, we are."

"About Noah's offer," Jenna told them. "I turned him down."

"Actually," Noah said, "Jenna came up with something better."

Jenna told them, "We want you to have five percent of the boat."

For the first time that day, every last vestige of their hostility just up and vanished.

Amos asked, "You're giving us five percent?"

Noah loved how this reason to smile reshaped his mouth, his face, his heart. Just loving it.

"No," Jenna said. "We're giving you five percent each."

"This boat, this project, what we do next," Noah said. "It all comes down to you. And us. Together."

Jenna said, "You know what I need to say. We simply don't have enough money to finish the rebuild."

Zia broke in with, "We can help."

"You're already helping," Noah said.

"Noah couldn't have come close to where we are without you guys," Jenna said.

"But that's not the issue," Noah said. "Well, okay, it's part of the issue. But you need to understand, after the rebuild comes the running costs. Insurance, fuel, upkeep, the list goes on and on."

"Rebuilding this boat has been a family affair," Jenna said. "That's what you are. Family."

"And that's how we need to decide on next steps," Noah said. "As a family."

The silence lasted until Amos started making tight little jerks. As if he was trying to suppress a cough. Or something.

Zia asked, "You got a bone in your throat?"

Amos wiped his eyes, said to his wife, "As far as apologies go, I'd say this is pretty much top of the list."

Aldana, however, was not done being grumpy. "It's a start."

Which was when Noah's phone chimed. He pulled it from his pocket, told Jenna, "It's Lane."

Zia asked, "Who?"

"Lane Pritchard," Jenna said. "By all accounts, not a good guy."

"But he's making a cash offer for the boat." Noah made the connection, said, "Lane, I'll need to phone you back. . . . Yes, all right. Today. No, I can't say exactly what time. As soon as we're done with something important."

When he lowered the phone, Jenna went on. "We don't know exactly what the offer would look like. Noah cut things off before we got that far."

"Actually, two offers," Noah said. "A straight buyout, and maybe talking a share."

"No. Please, not him as a partner."

Noah felt another smile take shape. "Are you asking or telling?"

"Whichever keeps that man at arm's length."

He said to the others, "Basically what it comes down to is, we could probably walk away with half a million after all our expenses. Maybe more."

"Enough to buy a nice, clean, reasonably-sized boat," Jenna said. "For all of us."

"No, absolutely not."

The response, coming from Zia's wife, surprised them all.

Briana was most comfortable in the background, a placid woman who quietly ran their family.

Zia asked, "Are you sure about that?"

"Am I sure? You ask me after all the time you've spent dreaming about your days on this boat?"

"Unfinished," Zia said. "Dry-docked sixty miles inland, and—"

"And nothing. Zia, honey, this is your *dream*. You tell your sons bedtime stories about where we're going. You've already got a photo of this boat on our wall. No. We're not selling. They can. But you're not. No."

Noah looked at his brother. "I'm assuming you'd like to sell."

"Well, you're assuming wrong." This from Aldana. "As usual."

Amos asked his wife, "Really? With two daughters planning on university? We need another expense—"

"No, Amos. With two daughters who talk about nothing else but getting on that boat and sailing to Fiji."

"Those islands are a little out of range."

"Don't you sass me. Don't you dare." Aldana pointed at Noah and Jenna. Holding hands. "Just because those two have gone all lovey-kissy-kumbaya doesn't mean I'm all out of venom."

"But . . . You hate boats."

"Correction. You and I both hate the sort of bouncy little smelly things. Not to mention that awful boat your pals can't be bothered to clean. Which is all we've ever been able to afford." She pointed to the boat partially shaded by the barn. "What do your daughters call that?"

"Their very own floating palace."

"See, I knew you could listen when you had to." She crossed her arms. "The answer is no. We're not selling."

Amos smiled. "Well, all right then."

"Are you laughing at me?"

"Not a chance in the whole wide world." He turned to Ethan. "What about you folks?"

"We're in for the long haul," Ryan said. "Right, hon?"

"Absolutely."

Amos turned back to his brother. "Why don't you start at the top and tell us what you know about this new money guy?"

CHAPTER 34

The next morning, Jenna woke with the sense that a band of tension and fear had become wrapped around her body during the night. It was still there when she parked in front of Noah's farmhouse at a quarter past six. Not a dominating force. But strong enough to drive a wedge between her and the man who smiled as he approached.

Noah must have noticed her distance, for he stowed his smile away and simply asked if she wanted a coffee for the road. When she declined, he held the door to his pickup, slipped behind the wheel, started south, and did not speak again until they joined the interstate below San Lu. And then it was only to ask if everything was okay.

She did not like how the tension seemed in control of both her and the pickup's atmosphere. She leaned against the door, trying to come to terms with her internal state, asking herself repeatedly the same question she had woken to repeatedly during the night: What did she actually want?

The answer was clear enough, though it frightened her to state it, even mentally. She wanted to love this man.

And she wanted to do so safely.

She wasn't after some sort of fairy-tale perfection. She simply wanted to know one thing. Could she rely on Noah not to run away again, give in to his own night terrors and break things off?

"Jenna?"

She knew it was time to speak, and said the first thing that came to mind. "I was thinking about Dino. You remember what my patients often said about time?"

"Sure. They thought they'd have more of it. I can't tell you how often I've circled back to that."

"Dino put it differently. The one occasion I pressed him about keeping his family outside the gates, he told me that time is a currency you've got stashed in a secret account. You can only spend it once. When it's gone, it's gone and it's never coming back. Your only choice is, how to spend it well."

Noah drove almost twenty miles down the freeway before responding. "I like the man's thought process. I'm not able to agree with his actions. How often was the guy married?"

"Just the one time, according to Zia's contact with the FBI. Dino arrived here with a wife and young daughter. A year or so later, she died in childbirth. He never remarried."

"So, just the two daughters. And their children. From them, there's not a single relative who loved him. Who wants to be with him for any other reason than to grab their share of his loot."

She nodded. "Exactly what I thought. And didn't say."

"That's sad." Another five miles, ten, the only sound coming from the wheels drumming along the highway. Then, "He needed secrecy to stay safe. But it's hard not to think this same attitude kept his family from ever getting close. I wonder if he was even aware of this."

"I wondered too."

"And?"

"I think he was proud of his secrets. Not just proud of staying safe. Proud of being his own man. He was the most fiercely independent person I've ever known. I liked him. But being his friend meant accepting him for who he was."

"Secrecy was what made him who he was." Noah's voice dropped a solemn octave. "For better or worse."

"Why does that make you sad?"

"Not sad. Not really. More ashamed." He glanced over. "I wasn't aware of what I let dominate my internal state. I ran away from knowing. I'm sorry it hurt you."

Jenna found the knot of tension tying her to the side door gradually beginning to unravel. "What's going to keep you from doing it again?"

She actually saw him shudder. "That frightens me. And worries me. So much."

He did not speak again. Nor did Jenna feel any need to press. There was a sense of comfortable release from her own tension, just hearing him admit to the prospect. Being willing to face the issues for which neither of them had answers.

At least, not yet.

She slipped over close enough to settle her hand upon his shoulder. "Your exit is coming up."

Santa Barbara County had some of the country's most restrictive zoning requirements. Several years back, torrential rains created a mudslide that tore down neighboring Montecito's main street. The river of mud and rocks and trees and cars destroyed scores of businesses, homes, hotels, and lives. Afterward the county relaxed its building requirements for a while.

Their destination was one of those structures that slipped under the wire. Four stories, the maximum permitted in central Santa Barbara. Spanish-style construction, carved wooden balconies, peaked central doors, painted tiles adorning the central walk, red-tiled roof. Central courtyard with a full Olympic-size pool. Carefully sculpted gardens, underground parking. Noah estimated there were twenty apartments. Four penthouses that must have cost a bomb. One of which was owned by the man they had come to see.

The instant Dino's grandson stepped through the front door, Noah had the guy pegged.

Auburn Raye reminded Noah of several wannabe directors he had worked for and disliked so much they made his teeth hurt. Flower-print aloha shirt, long hair professionally streaked, khaki shorts, Brazilian wish bands on both wrists, sunglasses dangling from a shell necklace. Eyes still puffy from whatever he had used the night before, expression set in what Noah assumed was a permanent scowl. He was probably aged in his early thirties, but sounded like a petulant teen when he demanded, "Who's this guy?"

Sol Feinnes walked a half step behind the grandson. The San Lu attorney took his time, shook Jenna's hand, then Noah's, before saying, "Allow me to introduce Noah Hearst, owner of your grandfather's boat. Ms. Greaves, of course, you already know. Noah, this is Auburn Raye."

"I thought you bought Grandad's boat." Then he spotted the federal agent rising from his nondescript four-door, and smirked. "Great. Let's get the party started."

Agent Wright Manley Banks wore what appeared to be the same slate-gray suit he had worn to the farmhouse. Sol made a solemn process of greeting the agent and saying, "I believe you know everybody."

With dark Ray-Bans masking his eyes, the agent's face held all the animation of a mannequin. "Why am I here?"

"Because I invited you." Sol turned to the grandson. "I sold your grandfather's boat to Mr. Hearst."

"Whatever." Auburn waved a vague hand toward the pool complex. "Let's get out of this heat."

When they were seated at a poolside table, Auburn demanded, "So I'm here. What now?"

"First, a correction," Jenna said. "Noah actually purchased your grandfather's boat from a police auction."

Auburn looked from Sol to Noah to Jenna. "This is interesting why?"

"Because," Jenna replied. "The boat was wrecked. And sunk."

Auburn laughed out loud. "Is this a joke?"

"No joke," Sol replied. "The police think the attackers used a sawed-off shotgun."

Auburn laughed a second time. "Good!"

Agent Banks asked, "You're not concerned?"

"Concerned? Man, I'm beyond thrilled. Grandad loved that boat twice as much as he did any of us. Ten times more." Auburn leaned back. Stretched out his legs. "I wish I had been there."

Jenna said, "Actually, I thought you were."

"That's why we're here? Because you thought I blew up Grandad's stupid boat?" Auburn laughed once more.

"No, I wanted to let you know that a very bad man has shown up. Just as soon as your grandfather's former identity became known."

But the young man remained captured by news about the boat. "You ask me, Aunt Eloise was behind it. She's always been the quietly vicious type."

"Someone went through there with an ax," Jenna pointed out. "Hard to do for a lady walking with a cane."

"That was probably compliments of cousin Willifred. What a dear boy that one turned out to be." He smirked at something unseen.

"What?"

"Oh, probably nothing. At least, nothing you can use."

"Tell me."

"Willifred's owned a string of boats."

Jenna resisted the urge to glance at Sol. "I never knew that."

"No reason you should have. Willifred plays things close to his chest. Which is the only reason he's not been arrested on multiple charges. I always suspected Willifred had no real interest in the sea. What he wanted was a chance to party away from prying eyes. Which is probably why dear old Grandad never once allowed Willifred to set foot on his precious vessel." Auburn stared over the pool's sparkling waters, then added, "Aunt Eloise went on for years about how the old man probably had a secret stash. And what do you know. She was right. Only not where she thought."

The agent asked Jenna, "This man making enquiries. Do you have a name?"

"Lane Pritchard. A supposedly retired LA lawyer."

"I've done some checking," Sol said. "LA police have long suspected him of being linked to the Mob."

Banks took out his phone. "Spell that name."

Jenna did so, then asked Dino's grandson, "Has he shown up here?"

"Not that I know of."

"Any chance he's been nosing around Dino's house?"

"How should I know?" Auburn jerked his chin in Sol's direction. "We keep waiting for the place to be sold."

"It was officially listed day before yesterday," Sol said. "The agent Dino instructed us to use now has three cash offers."

"You mean Benny Watts," Banks corrected.

"Legal records still show Dino Vicenza as owner," Sol replied. He looked at Auburn. "I must warn you. This question of identity may slow things down."

For the first time, Auburn showed real interest. "Does Mom know?"

"I've seen no need to involve Mrs. Raye," Sol replied. "Yet."

"She'll set the dogs to howling in Santa Cruz," Auburn said. "Mom's already burned through most of her inheritance. Bought some place in Kauai. It's either get her share of the house's sale or go on the hunt for another husband."

Noah felt like he stood outside himself, watching this drama from an objective distance. Close enough to hear everything that was said, but still well removed. Able to study this spoiled rich guy with the absurd name and wonder about the grandfather. How the old man had probably assumed his life was totally under control, long as his secrets kept him safe. How that mattered more than family.

He heard Jenna say, "We think Lane Pritchard might be after your grandfather's gold."

"Too late," Auburn replied. "My family can go through money fast as a California wildfire."

"I don't think," Jenna said, "this man will care."

"What's that supposed to mean?"

She gestured to the agent. "If he shows up asking questions, you need to alert Agent Banks. Immediately."

Banks asked, "Where is this gold now?"

"Mom's is mostly gone, like I said." Auburn looked from one to the other. "Mine's in a safety deposit box. What the others did with their shares, I have no idea."

Banks said, "I assume these assets have been duly reported to the IRS."

Sol replied, "That matter is between myself, my clients, and the proper authorities, and does not concern you."

Auburn looked at Jenna, his tone bitter. "This is your idea of revenge, bringing the feds down on my head?"

"The IRS is being handled," Sol repeated. "As I informed

you and all other family members. In any number of documents. Do be sure and let me know which I should resend."

Auburn smirked. "So many documents. So little time."

"Ms. Greaves is here as a courtesy. One that may save your life."

"Whatever." He rose to his feet. "Are we done?"

CHAPTER 35

Noah spoke just once on the drive from Santa Barbara to Morro Bay, and it was to say, "Sol called me last night. He wanted to make sure I knew what I was doing, giving the families five percent."

"Five percent each," she replied.

"Right. I told him it was the correct thing to do."

"What did he say to that?"

"Same as when I said you were to receive half plus the extra two percent." When he glanced over, Jenna thought she could see the glimmer of a smile in his gaze. "He hoped I was absolutely certain, because there was no way I could retract the step once I took it."

"That sounds like Sol."

He nodded. "I told him nothing I'd done in a long time felt this good."

The silence carried a comfortable note. Jenna started to speak several times, but nothing seemed as valid as reaching over and settling a hand on his shoulder.

As they wound their way around San Lu and took the road heading toward Morro Bay, Jenna found herself thinking back to her time with patients. Not any particular individual. All of them. Their faces fashioned a mental parade beyond the sunlit windshield. Their whispers drifted on the breeze through her open window.

Warning without words.

She knew the message. She saw it in their gazes. The tomorrow they would never have. The opportunity that was hers. Now. This very hour. The moment that came only once, and then was forever gone.

Jenna waited until they parked to ask, "What exactly are we doing here?"

"It's probably a waste of time," Noah replied. "But I'd like to see if we can help Wallace find a way out."

"Out of what, exactly?"

"I have no idea." He opened his door. "And it really doesn't matter."

She followed him across the almost-empty lot. "That almost makes sense."

The boatyard was surrounded by a rusting hurricane fence. The wide main gates were shut for the first time Jenna had ever seen. A makeshift CLOSED sign rattled in the hot breeze. Noah glanced around, then gestured for Jenna to step away. Three men walked up carrying fishing rods and coolers. They coded in a combination to the lock and slid the gates open. Noah followed them through and started across the silent yard.

In answer to her unspoken question, Noah said, "Wallace said he keeps a boat. I just wanted to check."

The forty-foot Hatteras was moored at the end of the pier farthest to the left. The boat's name, *Quick Getaway*, made a mockery of its silent state. Noah pointed to the shadow-figure shifting around inside, then called, "Wallace, it's Noah and Jenna."

"Go away."

"We want to help."

"That's simple enough. Sell Lane the boat."

"Can we come on board?"

A long silence, then, "It won't do any good."

Noah took that as their invitation and helped Jenna on board. He crossed the deck, knocked once, and stepped inside.

The cabin was littered with drink cans, empty bottles of cheap bourbon, local takeaway containers, and stained maps of the Mexican coast. Wallace watched them with red-rimmed eyes, tried for a sneer, and failed. "Come to see a dead man walking?"

"What does he have on you?"

"Wrong question." He lifted a half-full glass of something that had long lost its fizz. "The dice are loaded. The war's over, the good guys lost. The game is fixed. That's all you need to know."

Noah stood there, uncertain what to say. So Jenna asked, "Is there anything we can do to help?"

Wallace showed her a bottomless gaze, so empty the color of his eyes no longer mattered. "Different question, same answer. You don't give him what he wants, you'll find yourselves exactly where I am soon enough."

They left Morro Bay and followed the main road back inland. Noah skirted around San Lu and headed north on the Miramar Bay highway. Jenna was glad for the silence. She had seen Wallace's dark, hopeless gaze on some of her patients. Not many. Those who had it were the hardest to reach. They had lived with a true pessimist's bitter perspective. Facing death was for some a source of unending terror, but not most. The others, they took it as the ultimate confirmation. Jenna's attempts to be a friend in their final hours often met with bitter rejection.

For Jenna, the empty highway became adorned with the same faces she recalled on the trip from Santa Barbara. One patient after another flashed into view, as clear as the signs and structures they passed. Only now there was another one added to the mix. Wallace Myers. His bottomless gaze filled her with a silent desperation. A need to shout the words aloud.

I want to live.

But as she started to speak, Noah said quietly, "I think we're being followed."

Three minutes later, Jenna told Amos, "Noah made me call. I feel sillier than he did telling you about a noise in the dark."

"Not possible," Noah said.

"A dark Mercedes S-Class with a blanked-out windshield is tracking you north," Amos said. "You were right to call." Noah's phone was set on the middle console and connected to the pickup's speaker system. Jenna found a margin of comfort in how seriously Amos took this. "Read me the license."

She swiveled around and knelt on the seat. "California plates," she said, and read off the number.

As she started to swing back around, the car braked and swung left. "Wait, Amos. They've turned off."

"Just the same, you did right. I'll alert Zia."

"Amos, no. They're gone."

"Do you have a pen?"

"Yes."

He gave her a number. "That's Zia's private cell. I'll give him a heads-up."

"Amos—"

"Just in case, Jenna." He cut off.

Five minutes passed. Ten. Long enough for Noah to say, "Maybe I was wrong to say we should call."

"Amos didn't think so."

"Hang on." A long look in the rearview mirror. "They're back."

"What?"

"Don't turn around. Call Amos."

Soon as she started in, he asked, "Have you told Zia?"

"Not yet."

"Let me hook him in."

The seconds were fractured by her now-racing heart. Then Amos asked, "Zia, you on?"

"Read you five by five. Hi, Jenna honey."

Pulling a wayward lock of hair from her eyes revealed her trembly fingers. "Noah's here with me."

Amos said, "The Merc belongs to the Morino limo group out of LA."

"Doesn't ring a bell."

"I've got a buddy checking them out."

Noah said, "I should've thought to note the license plate of Lane's ride back at the house."

"Ancient history," Zia replied. "What are they doing?"

"Holding steady, about half a car length behind us," Noah said. "They basically fill my rearview mirror."

There was a deep-throated roar. Then Jenna cried, "There's *another one!*"

Noah said, "He's passed us. Come in directly in front—"

Amos shouted, "*Noah, pull off the road NOW.*"

Noah slammed on his brakes. Which was the only reason they were partly ready when the car in front hit his brakes so hard the tires smoked. The front Merc slewed slightly, then pulled off in front of Noah's truck.

Jenna shrilled, "He tried to get us to rear-end him!"

"Noah!"

"We're okay. We've halted. The Mercs have us hemmed in, not quite touching both bumpers. We're trapped."

"Zia?"

"Where are you at, Noah?"

"Just north of San Lu, headed home."

Jenna said, "I can see a sign for Regency Homes."

In reply, they heard Zia say, "All units be advised. Highway assault in process. Probable gang affiliation. Northbound on State Road 17, just past highway marker six. Victims are in a Ford F150 double cab. Assailants are driving two late-model Mercedes S-Class."

Jenna cried, "They're getting out!"

Noah said, "Five, no, six Latinos. Four from the front car, two from the rear . . . Wait, there's an old guy getting out of the rear car."

Amos demanded, "You getting this, Zia?"

"Roger that. Okay, Noah, three cars are inbound. Hang tight."

"Keep your hands visible at all times," Amos said. "Keep your phone on. Do *not* get out of your car."

Jenna turned and said, "The old guy is walking with a cane. Dark suit. Another younger guy in a suit but no tie is helping him."

"Here he comes," Noah said.

"They look very scary," Jenna said. Through her open window she heard the faint wail of sirens. "Thank God, oh thank God."

The old man gestured with the arthritic hand not holding his cane for Noah to roll down his window. Up close, the man's chin and one cheek and neck held a dark, leathery cast, like the skin of a human lizard. Jenna realized he had probably removed old tattoos by laser. The thought made her pulse race faster still.

The old man told Noah, "You did well there, young man. Avoiding that accident. Very well indeed."

Noah kept his hands on the wheel and did not respond.

"Such deadly accidents, they can come at you from any

direction. At any time. Of course you understand what I am telling you."

Noah did not respond.

The man tapped Noah's door with his cane. "I understand you have an item a dear friend of mine wishes to acquire."

The young man standing by his elbow said, "Boss, the sirens."

"I hear them." To Noah, "You would be well advised to accept my friend's offer. Avoid the risk of another more serious accident. Tell me you understand, Mr. Hearst."

When Noah did not reply, Jenna said, "We understand."

"Good. Very good. But I need to hear this from your friend here."

The sirens were screaming now. Several of them.

"Boss . . ."

The man tapped Noah's door. Harder this time. "You are fortunate to have such a wise companion, Mr. Hearst. Heed her counsel. For both your sakes." He allowed the young man to draw him away, only to turn back and call, "Do everything you possibly can to stay safe."

CHAPTER 36

Three and a half hours later, Jenna's blood was still fizzing when they gathered in Amos's home. It would have been much later, but Zia rushed the investigating detectives, refusing to permit them to take Noah and Jenna back to headquarters and try to ID the assailants. He insisted they be allowed to give their statements on the spot.

Ryan and Ethan arrived with Liam in tow. They filled the narrow dining room to bursting, while Aldana and her two daughters pulled things out of the fridge and made great heaping bowls of salads and finger food.

Jenna liked being surrounded by these people, these friends. They gradually helped settle her. What was more, they permitted her to feel weak and needy.

Noah remained locked in some internal dialogue, watching the conversation swirl around them, saying little. Reaching out every now and then, taking her hand. Connecting.

Then his phone rang. Noah checked the readout. "Unbelievable."

Jenna asked, "Who is it?" Knowing before he responded.

"Lane." Noah shook his head. "The nerve of that guy."

Amos reached out. "Want me to handle it?"

"I got it." Noah touched the connection. Listened a moment. Said, "Tomorrow." He listened a moment longer, then said again, "Tomorrow," and cut the connection.

Noah did not speak again while they ate. Midway through their salads, word came back from Amos's contact in LA. The Morino limo company was suspected to have Mob ties, probably used as a means of laundering cash. But there was nothing definite.

Noah and Jenna helped clear the table while the three police officers continued to dominate the conversation. After coffee and dessert were served and everyone was seated, Noah said, "I think we should sell the boat."

The room did not just go silent; if anyone blinked or breathed, Jenna could not tell.

Amos took the dessert spoon from his wife's immobile hand. "You're dripping."

Aldana looked at him. But for once his wife had nothing to say.

Noah said, "You all know how I came to be here in Miramar. Why I bought the boat. On the drive back from San Lu, this afternoon, it all came back to me. I was so *angry*. I left LA to *escape* all this. Now it feels like I'm back in the same old trap. Today was different, I know that. But in some respects it felt exactly the same."

Amos said, "We know what you mean."

"So here I am. Trying to rebuild this boat, my life, and it happens again."

Zia said, "Only this time, you've got friends on your side."

Ryan added, "And the law."

"You don't know what that means," Noah said. "The friendships, the sense of building a new home." He met Jenna's gaze. "A new life."

"And you want to sell?" Zia shook his head. "Sorry. You lost me."

"Because all this is more important than the boat."

Zia said, "We can protect you."

"Okay, yes, I get that. Just like you did today. For which I'm incredibly grateful. But that's not the point." He looked at Jenna. "Please tell me you understand."

Jenna had a great deal she wanted to say. But not just yet. She made do with a simple "Yes."

He held her gaze. "I won't take a step, *any* step, unless you agree."

"But it's not just me, is it?"

"No." He looked at the group. "This goes for all of you."

Aldana's elder daughter cried, "I *never* want to sell!"

"Honey, shush."

"Mom, you said—"

"Wait, sweetheart. No, don't leave. No storming off today." Aldana reached out. "Come here."

"I *love* that boat."

"We all do, sweetheart." She stroked her daughter's hair. "Go on, Noah."

"I love it too. I love the way our working together has brought it back to life, and me at the same time. At night, when it's just me and Bear and the boat and the dark, I think about going out. Traveling the open waters. Living aboard something that beautiful . . ."

He stopped. Stared at his hands. Jenna could feel his struggle. She shifted her chair closer. Settled her arm on his shoulders. Waited.

"I have to make a choice," Noah said. "I've seen firsthand and close up the cost of long, drawn-out battles. And that's really what I have to consider. After what happened today, would I ever feel safe? What happens if there's an accident, or an outright attack, and I lose one of you? No boat is worth that." He allowed Jenna to draw him closer still. "I think it's right to sell. But only if everyone agrees."

Aldana asked Jenna, "What about you? I haven't heard you say a single word about all this."

Jenna maintained her hold on Noah. "I haven't needed to. He's spoken for the both of us."

They planned well into the night, a noisy discussion dominated by the three police officers. Amos and Zia and Ryan worked it out in stages. Covering all the contingencies. Talking it through in calm bursts that Jenna found hard to follow. Like they were discussing things in a foreign tongue.

Jenna liked the charged atmosphere, how it unified the group. Even Liam and Amos's two daughters remained caught up in the tension, watching wide-eyed as they discussed how to best deal with a lawyer representing some very bad people. How to walk away. Safe and whole. Their lives and futures intact.

Half an hour later, Noah phoned Lane back and suggested he come up the next afternoon. They then walked down the valley road to the farmhouse. Everybody came.

Amos pulled her slightly to one side, and said, "You don't have to do this."

"It's a very good plan. And I want a role to play. A real part."

"This is as real as it gets. Putting you on point means we can hopefully keep this perp from getting nervous. He can deliver his message, then leave without anybody getting in his face. No harm, no foul."

The others walked a ways behind them, close enough for Jenna to hear Noah's voice, but not be able to understand what he said. Zia responded, causing the others to laugh out loud. The first such sound that night. Jenna said, "This is exciting. Despite everything."

Amos chuckled. "You should have been a cop."

"Thanks, but I'm happy with my chosen profession."

They did not speak again until they stood by Jenna's car. Amos said, "If you change your mind . . ."

She patted his arm. "Not happening."

The farewells took forever. When they were done, Jenna was stationed by Noah's side, their arms tight around each other. She could feel the day's tension still held him, that and the decision he had made about the boat. The night enveloped them in a warm silence. The wind had stilled, and the sky overhead was a silver wash. When the headlights drifted away and the valley was still, Noah said, "It's not too late."

"You don't really mean that."

"Don't I?"

"No, it's regret talking."

"Do you have any?"

"Of course. I probably always will. But you were right, what you said." She swept a hand out, taking in the valley and all their departed friends. "What we have here is far too precious to risk over a boat."

"What *we* have."

"Yes."

He held her a moment longer, then said, "Coming close to losing you was what made me realize there was really no choice here. This is all too valuable. Too precious. I've been given a second chance at life. I need to do my best to work things out right this time."

Which left Jenna with such a grand feeling she lifted her face and kissed him. Again. "One voice, two hearts. That's how it feels, listening to you talk."

CHAPTER 37

Lane Pritchard arrived precisely at four the next afternoon.
He traveled in the same dark Mercedes S-Class, driven by
the same immobile driver hidden behind the same heavily
tinted windshield. Lane rose from the rear seat, stretched,
and took a moment to survey the scene. Three police cars
were parked to either side of his vehicle, plus Noah's pickup
and Jenna's car. Amos stood on the platform, his back to the
farmhouse. At the boat's stern, Aldana and Ryan sorted piping and bathroom fittings on a trestle table. There was the
sound of a precision saw and quiet conversation. Jenna stood
alone by the porch stairs. Waiting.

She had not slept more than a couple of hours. Her eyes
felt grainy. Her upper body ached from tension she could
not release. She had spent most of the night reliving the attack, feeling the helpless terror sweep over her. Whenever
she managed to push that away, there they were. The faces of
her former patients. All the way back to her late sister. The
one whose dream she was about to let go.

Time and again she started to call Amos. Tell him she wasn't the one to handle this situation, meet the man representing the unseen killers. Ask the professional law-enforcement officer to take over. The electric thrill she'd felt walking the valley road alongside Amos was gone now. She felt childish for even having volunteered. As if she'd been buoyed by the presence of three cops, people who spent their entire adult lives dealing with such hazards. But every time she reached for her phone, something held her back. She could not explain it. Only that it remained important for her to be the one.

Lane approached Jenna and offered a meaningless smile. "We were not properly introduced."

"Jenna Greaves."

"Of course. You served as nurse to the boat's original owner. Wallace spoke very highly of you."

"I prefer the term caregiver."

"Terms are so very important, are they not? The late gentleman's family uses other terms to describe you."

She decided there was nothing to be gained by continuing that line of conversation. "Work on the wiring has reached a critical point. Noah asked me to greet you."

"I am honored and grateful both. Wiring?"

"They're finished with the flying bridge." She pointed to where two shadow figures worked. "The second set of controls, in the pilot's cabin on the main deck, have to work in precise tandem. They're calibrating the two systems."

"Are you a boat person, Ms. Greaves?"

"I better be. I own a 42.5 percent share. Same as Noah."

Lane showed angry surprise, but recovered swiftly. "And the other fifteen percent?"

Jenna motioned to the three cop cars. "Five percent to each of our other partners. Amos Prior, Sheriff of Miramar County. Detective Ryan Eames, Miramar police. And Zia Morales, senior detective in San Luis Obispo."

This time, his rage could not remain under wraps. Cold, implacable. He gestured angrily at the car. Immediately the driver emerged, a stone-faced killer in black.

Soon as the driver started toward them, Amos began descending the steps. Jenna showed him an open palm. Amos didn't like it, but he stopped. And remained standing there. On full alert.

The driver held a small pack, perhaps twice the size of a cell phone. He swept it over her, hairline to T-shirt to jeans. "Clean."

"Wait in the car." When the driver retreated, Lane said, "You are sadly mistaken if you think this show of force would impress me. Much less the people I represent."

Jenna remained silent.

"Accidents can happen, Ms. Greaves. Far removed from any jurisdiction. Out to sea, in a boat repaired by people who have no experience whatsoever in such work."

Abruptly, Jenna took a giant mental step away from the night's worry, the tension and fears and regret. All of it miles removed from where she stood. She was now enveloped by the same calm distance that had shielded her through so many hard hours.

This was why she was the one dealing with Lane Pritchard, she realized. Why she had felt so certain she needed to do this. The others would confront. Do what this man probably expected. React with anger. And be defeated in the process.

Lane took her silence as reason enough to continue. "Believe me when I tell you, Ms. Greaves. The people I represent will have this boat." He lowered his face until she could watch her dual expressions in the lenses of his sunglasses. "They're going to have *everything*."

She held her ground. Untouched by his ire. "I don't understand. They know about the secret safe in the home's cellar. That gold has mostly been spent. Not to mention how the boat was searched and sunk. If there was anything more to be found, which I doubt, it's gone now."

Her calm clearly unsettled him. He leaned away. Studied her from a different angle. "That is not of your concern."

"So . . . It's a matter of pride."

"Pride, revenge, their motives are not the issue here. Your survival is."

She breathed around the sensation that Millie had joined her. Her sister was part of this now. Without regret or any sense of remorse. As clear a message as Jenna could possibly receive that she was doing the right thing. "Make your offer."

His rage was gone now. Erased by how she remained untouched. Unscathed. Distant. "One and a half million dollars. Cash."

"No. Sorry."

"Did you not hear a word I said?" But Lane's tone was different. Almost petulant. A man not accustomed to having his power denied. "These people, they will have—"

"I get all that. But look at what you're facing here." She pointed to the boat. "Three senior officers. People with clout in their agencies. People who could make a lot of trouble for you and your clients. Which means your offer needs to be high enough to satisfy my partners. Keep them from asking questions. One point five doesn't even cover our costs."

He inspected her anew. "Name your price."

"Three."

"Impossible."

"Three would be enough—"

"Out of the question." He leaned in. Quiet now. "Listen carefully, Ms. Greaves. There is a point beyond which my clients will go silent. Stop with the warnings. You understand?"

There was a faint shimmer to the air between them, a moment where her protection almost dissolved. Then, "So you tell me."

He took a long moment, then replied, "Two point two five. That is my last offer. And your final chance to walk away intact."

CHAPTER 38

Three nights later, it was all in place. Sol phoned to confirm the funds had been transferred into their joint account. Payment in full.

Wallace was scheduled to arrive around noon the next day, accompanied by his crane and tractor-trailer truck. There to cart away their boat.

Noah and Jenna took turns phoning Amos and Zia and Ryan. Letting them know it was happening as scheduled. Asking them to come. Jenna thought they both sounded rather formal, but there was no helping the tone, or the sorrow most of them showed at being invited to a party they had no interest in attending. But they were coming. All of them. To be part of this façade. Show Lane what he needed to see. Make sure everyone stayed safe. Meet whatever came next together.

They drove into town, stopped by Noah's favorite Mexican for takeaway. Brought it back and ate it on the rear porch, with stars and a slumbering Bear for company. And the boat. Their vessel seemed larger in the dark, a great half-finished sculpture resting quietly beneath its shelter.

Jenna was the one who actually said the words. "You know what I'd like to do?"

Noah was watching her, his gaze shining in the dark. "I think so, yes."

"Tell me."

In response, he rose and bundled up their remnants and took them inside. When he emerged, he carried blankets and sheets and pillows and flashlight. "Ready?"

"Yes. Let's."

They crossed the rear yard and entered the barn. The air smelled of varnish and sawdust and paint. They climbed into the boat, crossed over the nearly finished deck, and entered the second largest suite, which was located on the bow's port side, just ahead of the galley. This section had received the least damage: a few cracks in the flooring, easily repaired, shelves ripped out and now replaced, mattress sliced open and tossed. The window had not yet been resealed, and a cool night breeze pushed through. Noah dumped the bedding on the empty frame and left. Jenna was making up two pallets when he returned with the one battery lamp that still functioned. "I wish we had a bottle of wine."

"Another time. One that doesn't hold so much baggage."

"Right." He set the lamp on the side table and cut off the flashlight. "Tired?"

"Exhausted. Long days."

He lay down, waited until she was settled. Watched her a long moment. "I better cut off the lamp, else we'll be sharing our room with all kinds of flying night creatures."

"All right." She felt him settle down beside her. She knew she could ask for intimacy. But she was glad he did not press. Now simply wasn't the time. She felt he knew that too, the way he turned on his side and watched her in the gloom, eyes shining, comfortable with just being here. In this moment. Sharing the half-finished dream. She said, "We're going to have a boat."

"We are. Yes."

"And we're going to tour any number of foreign lands."

"Jenna, we can go wherever you want." He lay on his back, staring at what was still to come. "We can get an outstanding boat for about two thirds of what we have. Save the rest for running costs. Parcel it out so the others have their share of funds to do whatever they please."

She was tempted to slip over, lay her head on his chest. But there was something she needed to say. Something that required a fractional distance. Far enough to say, "Before the attack. When we left Wallace's boat. I've seen his attitude before. Grim. Defeated. No hope, and determined to hold on to this bleak vision until the very end." She turned onto her back. Reliving that moment. "I felt like I couldn't breathe. Like he sucked the life and hope right out of me. When we got in the car and started back, all I could think was, I want to live."

She heard the rustling of his pallet, felt the underlay move as he rose to a seated position. She could see the gleam of his eyes. Feel the strength and caring of this good man. She said it again, "I want to live."

"Your job?" he asked. "Your calling?"

"I want that too. Long as I can hold on to life. Death is a part of everything. Just like change. So much of our futile struggle comes down to trying to push our way out of both. Which is worse than foolish."

"Like tomorrow."

"I was so proud of what you said to the others. I didn't know if you would be able to see beyond everything you'd been through in LA. I thought I'd have to walk you through it when we were alone. When you told them what you did . . ." She looked up at him. "I love you, Noah."

He reached for her hand. Held it with both of his. Silent. Sharing the impossible hour. Together.

She asked, "What about you?"

"I've thought about this a lot. I'm not ready to go back to LA. I don't know if I ever will. But I love building. Love handling a crew, taking on major projects."

"You're good at it."

"Amos and I had a quick chat. And Sol. This old place is up for sale. I'm thinking of taking it on. They've agreed to help put together a finance package. I'd like to turn this into a weekend getaway for somebody who's made it to the top. Hold on to the old-timey feel. Transform everything except the outer shell into the highest possible quality. Add a covered terracotta walkway, possibly wall it in like an extended atrium, running back to the barn. Turn that into an atelier, art studio, cinema room, pool house, whatever."

"A work of art."

He lay back down. Snuggled in close. Stared at the ceiling together. For what seemed like hours. Until Jenna said, "Can I ask you something?"

"Anything."

"A boat like this. What are the running costs?"

"Jenna, you're asking the wrong guy. I've never even owned a boat."

"But you've checked."

"Well, sure. What I've heard, it varies tremendously. How far you're traveling, the number of guests, the quality of things like wine and booze. And crew. Then there's insurance, regular maintenance, dockage. Those are the big-ticket items on a boat like this."

"Ballpark."

"Okay, say it's just us and a few guests. No extra crew. We hold to cruising the west coast." He was silent, thinking. Then, "Call it three, maybe four thousand dollars."

"Per day?"

"Per day that the boat's in use. Yeah, something like that. At a minimum." He turned toward her. "Where are you going with this?"

"I was just thinking about the money Dino left me."

"Fifty thousand dollars."

"Plus the money I earned watching the house."

"Which you sunk into this craft. And which you are getting back. Every penny."

"That's not . . . It isn't like Dino to hand over a gift like this boat and not factor in the running costs. Which I couldn't afford in the best of circumstances." She sat up. Crossed her legs. "Thinking out loud here."

"Go for it."

"Dino insisted I be there for the reading of his will. Which made no sense. But something he had written in there . . ."

"About what?"

"The secret safe. That it was hidden behind a panel, in the deepest part of his special home. Below his fuel."

Noah sat up. Facing her. "For real?"

"Dino loved his wine. Right to the very end. But he never called it that. Fuel. Not ever."

Noah watched her. "You thinking . . ."

"I don't know. Maybe."

He was already moving. "Let's go see."

CHAPTER 39

It was a clear, crisp night, but the bilges still held some of the previous day's heat. Ethan's newly finished main floor rested on a repaired fiberglass sheet that formed the bilge's ceiling. The open space ran from the engine room's reinforced wall all the way to the bow. Down here, the yacht's full size was evident. A huge space, made larger by the low ceiling. Jenna could walk upright so long as she stood next to the tanks. Noah had to crouch.

She knew the fuel tanks served as a major part of the ship's ballast, the weight that helped keep the boat stable. These tanks ran the entire length of the boat, gradually diminishing in size as they approached the bow. They looked like massive whitewashed chests, with flat, stable walkways about fourteen inches wide running down either side.

The boat's lights were not hooked up. Noah gave her the flashlight and took the battery lamp as he crawled to the tank's other side. "What are we looking for?"

"I have no idea."

"Tell me what you found at the house."

"A secret safe. Hidden right where he said it would be, behind the central panel. Above it were the wine racks."

"So let's start in the center and work back. Then forward." He moved forward. "How did the panel come off?"

"I pressed on it. Hard. I really had to shove." She shifted position to stay opposite him. "This is probably a total waste of time."

"What else have we got to do tonight?"

"Sleep."

Noah crouched down, disappearing from view. "Okay, there's that."

Jenna knelt on the walkway and studied the foundation connecting the tank to the hull. Instantly she saw there was ample room to hide a drawer safe. A ten-inch fiberglass ledge ran the entire length of the tank. She ran her hand over the rough surface, searching, pressing. She tried to tell herself that Dino probably thought the boat was gift enough, she needed to work out for herself how to keep it going . . .

Jenna heard a faint click. Then Noah called, "I found it."

CHAPTER 40

The next day, Wallace Myers returned.

He and his team used the same portable crane to lift the boat off its wooden supports and settle it back on the tractor-trailer. The boat shone like a massive white jewel in the sunlight.

Lane Pritchard's Mercedes was parked nose out, facing back down the valley road. The driver remained stationary behind the wheel, the motor running. Lane made circuits of the barn and backyard. He continually supervised Wallace loading the boat. But Jenna was fairly certain it was all pretense. Lane cast too many glances their way. Using his sunglasses to hide the way he inspected them in turn. Amos and Aldana, their two girls. Zia and Briana and their sons. Noah, Sol, Ethan, Ryan, Liam. And Jenna. Studying them intently. Searching for cracks.

Sol's wife was named Rachel, a pediatric surgeon working out of San Lu's main hospital. She was a tall, angular woman with sharply intelligent features and a wealth of dark hair.

She drew Jenna away from the crowd, walked them out to the road, said, "I'm sorry for speaking with you on such a day. And again for being blunt. But I've received a call, a young boy was struck by a baseball just below his heart. He's having difficulty breathing."

Jenna liked having a reason to turn away. "I understand."

"Sol has spoken highly of you. For years. I wish we had met before now. And in better circumstances." She waved that aside. "Our hospital is facing a very serious shortage of experienced nurses. I was wondering if by any chance you might be thinking about staying. Putting down roots."

She saw Lane inspecting them and thought, *Look all you like.* "I haven't really considered it. But . . ."

"Yes?"

"To tell you the truth, everything is up in the air right now."

She nodded. "Why don't you come down, let me show you around. We'll have lunch."

"Thank you. I'd like that."

She offered Jenna her card. "I'm working days all next week." And started for her car.

Jenna walked back to where Noah stood on the porch. He asked, "What was all that about?"

"Later." She saw how Aldana had taken up position by the trestle tables, her arms around her daughters, both of whom wept silently. She saw how Lane studied the women, then went back to surveying Wallace at work. Jenna was beyond glad they had not said anything. To anyone.

Amos and Zia and Ryan stood together, arms crossed, gazes hard as granite. Liam sat next to where Ethan stood. Grim. Sad.

Perfect.

This was the only version Lane Pritchard was allowed to see. The only way they would ever be safe. The tragic loss. The defeat. The sorrow. He would go away satisfied.

Noah held Jenna's hand until it was over. But as Wallace climbed into the truck cab and Lane started toward his Mercedes, Noah called out, "Wait!"

Noah walked to the boat in its mobile cradle. He reached up, placed a hand on the boat's stern . . .

And just stood there.

Finally, Jenna couldn't bear it any longer. She approached him, gripped him with both arms, and settled her head on his shoulder. After a moment, she said, "It's time to let go."

CHAPTER 41

They needed six weeks to put it all in place.

Six weeks of planning, talking, working through mounds of documents, spending hours and hours in Sol's conference room. Watching it take shape. Become real.

The summer ended. The girls and Liam and Zia's sons were back in school. Routines were reset.

They met with Amos's family, but not often. They occasionally spoke by phone with the others. The shadow of the empty barn was with them wherever they reached out. And it was too hard for Jenna and Noah not to say anything. Waiting was necessary. But so very hard just the same.

Distribution of Lane's payment had never been discussed. By some silent accord, the others took their signal from Noah and Jenna. They waited.

The first Saturday after Labor Day, they met for dinner at Castaways, Miramar's premier restaurant. The owner had recently taken what before had been a wine cellar and transformed it into a private dining alcove. Jenna and Noah arrived first. They had been spending more and more time together, moving gradually from two people who cared for each other to becoming a couple in love.

They greeted each of the arriving families, playing host and hostess for the evening. Sol came alone, apologizing for yet another emergency that required Rachel to stay at the hospital. Otherwise they were all present, including Liam and Zia's boys and Aldana's two daughters.

A brass chandelier dangled from the high ceiling. But most of the room's illumination came from candles set in alcoves that lined three walls. The flagstone floor and carved shelving dated back to the nineteenth century, and glowed softly in the flickering light. Jenna and Noah directed everyone into place around the oval table, taking seats directly across from each other.

Trying not to smile.

Their waiter served champagne, soft drinks for the young ones. Then a first course of grilled California artichokes with Serrano ham. Gradually the room's atmosphere brightened. When laughter encircled the table, Jenna said, "I think it's time."

"You do it," Noah said.

"Are you sure?"

He signaled the waiter, asked that they not be disturbed, then told Jenna, "Please."

"All right." To the table, "We have some news."

Aldana clapped her hands. "You're engaged! I told Amos it had to be something special."

"It's not that," Jenna said, watching the man seated across from her. "Not yet."

Noah pretended to swoon. "My poor heart just went pitter-pat."

Aldana said, "Then what is it?"

"Let the lady speak," Amos said. "Maybe we'll find out."

Jenna turned to Sol. "The envelopes, if you please."

"My sincere pleasure." He passed out three buff folders.

"There are quite a few papers for you to sign," Jenna said. "But the one thing on top can't wait."

They pulled out the documents, gaped at what was paper-clipped on top.

Three checks.

A hundred and twelve thousand, five hundred dollars. Each. Five percent of the total sales price.

"Sol is coming in as our partner," Jenna said. "Which means your share of the sale is now free and clear."

Zia said, "So . . . We're not getting a new boat?"

"The lady just said Sol is partnering with us," Amos told him. "What do you think that's all about?"

"Tell you the truth, I'm trying to pick myself off the floor."

"We're setting up a trust," Jenna said. "The trust will serve as the new boat's owner. Those papers represent your joint ownership of the trust."

"Sol has been very generous," Noah said. "His participation means we can share the wealth. And still buy a boat."

Zia waved the check like a fan. "Don't get me wrong. This money, it's college for our boys. But I don't understand . . ."

Amos said, "You've found a boat. Tell me I'm wrong."

"And what a boat it is," Sol said.

"Only if you agree," Jenna said. "This has to be a unanimous decision."

"But we figure it's such a good deal, we went ahead and cut you checks for your full share." Noah smiled at her. "Jenna found it. My job was to agree."

She reached into her purse and came out with six full-color catalogs. "It's a Princess 72. Almost brand-new."

"The first owners took possession," Sol said, "and four weeks later were required to declare bankruptcy. The boat has become part of the court's seizure of assets."

"Fifty-two hours on the motors," Noah said.

"With Sol's participation, we have enough left over to cover running costs for the next two years."

"This has to be unanimous," Noah said. "Otherwise it's dead in the water."

"Bad joke," Jenna said. "Terrible."

"But funny, right?"

"Okay, maybe a little." To the others, "We think this is the right move, but only if you all agree."

Zia rose to his feet. Lifted his glass. "Here's to having a reason to celebrate."

Amos stood beside him. "To friends. Good times. And family. And a new boat that I will learn to enjoy."

CHAPTER 42

Their fond farewells carried them out into the street, where they stood and laughed and chattered until after midnight. Finally fatigue and the children forced them to part ways. Noah spoke softly with his brother, shook his hand, then came back up to where Jenna waited. "He and Aldana will join us directly."

They had debated this for weeks. And decided that, really, they had no choice.

Noah's brother had to know.

And if Amos, then Aldana. That was how it was between them.

Jenna had a fresh pot of coffee ready when they arrived. They took up stations on the back porch, mugs in hand. Noah said it again. "Please, Jenna. You do this."

She took it slow. Enjoying how Noah chipped in from time to time. Making their final night on the boat live again.

She started with their conversation in the forward cabin. Recalling Dino's will. The hunt . . .

"You found it, didn't you?" Amos said. "A second safe."

"We did. Yes."

Aldana asked, "More gold?"

"No." She reached into her pocket, drew out the velvet satchel. It had probably been black at some point, but age and damp from the boat's sinking had turned it an uneven beige. She waited while Noah set the battery lamp on the small table, then untied the drawstrings, and said, "Hold out your hands."

She spilled out . . .

Diamonds.

"One to three carats," Noah said. "The five stones Sol checked are all first quality. These sizes are apparently the easiest to translate into ready cash."

Aldana selected one from her husband's palm, her fingers trembling. "How many?"

"Three hundred."

"If they're all the same quality," Noah said, "we're talking somewhere around twenty-five million dollars."

"Perhaps more, according to Sol," Jenna said. "A lot more."

Noah said, "You know what comes next."

Jenna liked how it was Aldana who said, "No one can ever know. For the sake of our daughters and everyone else."

"We have to assume they're watching," Jenna said. "For how long is anyone's guess."

"Which is where Sol's help becomes vital," Noah said.

"The trust serves as a blind," Jenna said. "All expenses in regards to our boat are paid through the accounts that Sol handles. Running costs, maintenance, insurance, the works. Sol is officially counting this as part of his investment."

Jenna took back the diamonds, poured them into the satchel. "We have a safety deposit box for these babies. Which is registered by the trust, and with you two as co-signatories."

"And for the time being, that's where they'll stay," Noah

said. "But if anything happens, to you or any of the others, it's there. Waiting. Hopefully we won't need them. But it's our backup. Just in case."

"Sol has assured us he can handle any necessary sale discreetly," Jenna said. "And any new income to the trust will be tax free."

"Sol says this falls under the federal laws dealing with lost property," Noah said. "Which means there is no obligation to disclose these funds to the federal government."

"Just the same," Jenna warned. "We have to remain very cautious. We need to make sure there's no reason for watchers to become aware of what we found."

"No," Aldana agreed. "That can't happen."

"The longer we wait, the better," Noah said.

Amos asked, "And the safe?"

"Gone," Noah said. "Stripped out. The base is now a solid fiberglass and resin block. Same as all the others."

The silence lasted until Amos said, "Thank you for trusting us."

"You're family," Noah said. "We wouldn't have it any other way."

CHAPTER 43

Three afternoons later, they headed south on the San Lu highway, then took the turning for Morro Bay.

They stopped by a cantina that catered to the beach crowd. They left the town by way of the meandering lane through the nature preserve, past the old-growth forest of pines and Pacific cypress, down to Shell Beach.

A family with two preschool children and an Irish setter played in the calm waters. Otherwise the crescent-shaped beach was theirs.

Jenna had not returned since bringing Dino's boat up from the Santa Barbara marina, all those many eons ago. The dock was fronted by a high metal fence rimmed with spikes. The gate combination was Dino's birth date, which was good for a shared smile.

The landing was flanked by large rusting cabinets sunk in a concrete foundation. They walked down the long pier, out to where the cove's sheltered waters surrounded them. They ate in silence, sharing their meal with gulls who danced upon the sunset.

Finally, Jenna said, "We need to talk about tomorrow."

Noah settled his back against the nearest piling. "All right."

"I've been asked to take on a new patient."

"Where?"

"Seattle."

"That's quite a ways away."

"Yes."

"How long?"

"Impossible to say. It could be as long as three or four months."

"Or nineteen."

"No, Noah. Not ever again."

"Just the same, Jenna, I will miss you terribly."

She nodded. "I've met with Sol's wife. She's offered me the position of head nurse in her surgical unit."

When Noah did not respond, she said, "Tell me what you're thinking."

"Jenna, I never want to come between you and your calling. But three months . . ."

"I know."

"I really don't think I should say more than that."

"I understand."

A gull flitted down, graceful as a feathered ballerina. Noah tossed a final bit of bread, and together they watched it dance away on wings turned molten by the sunset. "What was your late sister's name?"

"Millie," she replied. "That's so strange."

"What?"

"I was just thinking about her. While we ate I had the strongest sense Millie was here with us. She always loved her sunsets."

"Millie would be a great name for our boat," he said. "That is, if you and the others agree."

She reached over and settled her hand on his.

"Let's get married," she said.

Because it was time.